MYTH OF OMEGA

Zoey Ellis writes dark-edged fantasy romances described by readers as 'intensely erotic' and 'unputdownable.' A Londoner, cat mama, and proud romance and epic fantasy addict, Zoey loves possessive heroes, sexual tension that jumps off the page, and memorable, magical worlds. Visit her online home for more media and updates about her books and author journey: www.zoeyellis.com

~Also by Zoey Ellis~

The Last Dragorai
A Lair So Sinful
A Lair So Loyal
A Lair So Primal
A Lair So Fateful

Beholden Duet
A Savage Debt
A Tainted Claim

Myth of Omega

Crave To Conquer #1
Crave To Capture #2
Crave To Claim #3

Reign To Ruin #4
Reign To Ravage #5
Reign To Rule #6

Own To Obey #7
Own To Obsess #8
Own To Obtain #9

Empire of Angels
Claimed By Power #1
Ruined By Power #2
Awakened By Power #3

CRAVE

—◄ TO ►—

CONQUER

ZOEY ELLIS

Crave To Conquer, Myth of Omega Book 1
Copyright © Zoey Ellis 2018. All rights reserved
www.zoeyellis.com

Zoey Ellis Books
ISBN: 978-1-912931-18-7

First Edition: January 2018

LOX EMPIRE
Formally known as the Eastern Lands
WHITE OCEAN
RAYDELMORE
HALLOWCRYST
MISBURY
GRENCE
OTHLLAND
GRENCE STRAIT
LOX PALACE
ARIYON
NEKA
ASHENS
NEKA ISLES
FENGAR
FENGISH SEA
ARIYON SEA
CILLFORD
RICSFORD
JYNORA
VAMORIAN BAY
SADERTHORNE
DORLI
VAMORE
THE WASTELANDS
ISLANDS OF ASHENS
COPYRIGHT © 2018 BY ZOEY ELLIS

CHAPTER ONE

DROCCO

Drocco glared into the eyes of the traitor as he severed his head.

The squelch, pop, and ripping of flesh and ligaments filled the Great Hall as Drocco's dagger tore through the man's neck. His vast army of Alphas, the Lox, packed out the entire space from wall to wall, their fury made obvious by the burn in their eyes and the growled curses they muttered.

The traitor, an Alpha himself, had been bold enough to grit his teeth and keep his grunts low, trying to avoid screaming, but by the time Drocco's dagger scraped bone, his voice was hoarse. He had been one of Drocco's most fearsome warriors and yet a bitter hatred had appeared in his eyes when the truth about his loyalty was revealed. That hatred stained his expression in death, permanently declaring his true feelings for Drocco and the Lox.

Finally, Drocco lifted the man's head into the air, as his body dropped to the ground. The hall erupted into a vicious cheer as his warriors pumped their fists and yelled out in triumph. Shouts also came from the surplus of Alphas that spilled out into the corridors surrounding the hall.

Drocco held still, allowing the man's stinking blood and slime to slosh down his arm and splatter onto the raised platform he stood on. "This man has been with us for six months," he bellowed into the noise. "He has been a member of the most feared, most revered, most skilled army known to all Lands. He has trained with us, fought with us, learned from us." He paused to look around the hall. "He has been privy to powerful strategies that resulted in some of our most successful victories. And he was a traitor!" Drocco's roar soared across the enormous hall. Silence pressed over the hall now, all eyes fixed on Drocco up on the platform.

"His death is not a victory. This betrayal reflects badly on all of us! We are Lox. We do not abide traitors. Not for one day, let alone six fucking months! All of you are responsible for this man remaining undetected for so long."

He could almost feel the seven hundred Alphas before him bristle in unison. It was the first time he had implied that they were at fault for any traitors found among them, but he was not going to let it slide this time. As an army of over twelve thousand, they all had to be vigilant. He specifically looked along the front of the crowd where his generals stood. They each secured a territory in the expansive Eastern Lands Drocco had conquered and each had a Lox division they were responsible for. They needed to be aware that Drocco had seen their faces at this briefing.

"We do not know what information has gone to the Western Lands," he continued to bellow. "We do not know what they plan for us. We have only just secured the Eastern Lands and it will be stripped from us if we cannot protect ourselves from these underhanded tactics by deviants across the White Ocean. Under my leadership, we have conquered every city, every territory, and every district that I promised. We are here, Alphas. We have made it. I have done it.

"But I also made you a vow when the Lox formed. A vow that would ensure you live full and complete lives as the Alphas you deserve to be and I cannot fulfill that vow if I'm being targeted from within my own ranks."

The hall was so still it was as though the Alphas before him were statues. He threw the man's dripping head to one side.

"All warriors need to be watched carefully by each of us. Anything suspicious should be reported. You know the culture by which we live and if a man is not a part of it, he doesn't belong here, traitor or not. I do not expect to be spending my time dealing with this shit again within the next six months."

A ripple of nods moved through the crowd and many pushed their chests up and widened their stances. Drocco suspected some of them thought he questioned their loyalty and abilities, and in a way, he did. It wasn't enough to be a ruthless Alpha—that wasn't the only thing that set them apart from other armies. They had to be intelligent too. Alphas were capable of both, and any Alpha in his army needed to be, as a matter of requirement, or they might as well die with the traitors.

Drocco stepped to the edge of the platform. "We are the only Alpha army in existence. If we fall to the stereotype pressed upon us, we are no better than those we deem unworthy of the name Lox." He let the words hang in the air for a long moment before adding, "I am contemplating whether to still move forward with the celebration planned at the turn of the season. I'm not sure it's deserved."

He stalked off the platform to the servants holding the large bowl of water to wash his hands and arms. As he soaped up, the warriors remained silent. His commander, Torin, approached, his gray eyes searching Drocco's face. Drocco ignored him. He already knew Torin would think he had gone too far in basically accusing them of treason, but he didn't care. Another servant gave him a towel to dry with and he left the Great Hall without another word.

The Alphas filling the surrounding corridors parted for him and soon he marched along an empty passageway. Torin, who had followed him from the hall, kept pace beside him. At Torin's insistence, and Drocco's annoyance, Lox guards followed him wherever he went, but in the palace they stayed further behind.

"Was he the last?" Drocco asked without looking at him, his voice hard.

"For now, yes," Torin replied.

"For now?" Drocco almost barked. "I want all of Malloron's spies, like that one, out of my Empire. Permanently."

"It is impossible to detect them when we don't understand the Talent, Drocco," Torin said wearily, like he had done many times before.

Drocco stopped abruptly, turning to look Torin in the eye. "That excuse is wearing thin, Torin. If we cannot protect the Empire from that asshole, we don't deserve to keep it. I don't want the Talent to even exist in my Empire and certainly not in my palace. Those who manipulate magic can never be trusted, and that is the only way that bastard operates. Find a way to get rid of his fucking spies."

Torin dipped his head in a nod. "I will, Drocco."

Drocco held his eye for a moment. Torin was the only one permitted to call him by his first name, and the only person he truly trusted and confided in. Having known each other since childhood, Torin had weathered all aspects of Drocco's mood and yet still remained by his side. Drocco had never known Torin to let him down but leading an army was not the same as running an Empire. He needed to consider that Torin may not be up to this job. He was a Beta, after all.

Torin seemed to read his gaze. "It will be done," he insisted.

Drocco turned and continued down the corridor. "I'm going to the training grounds."

"The historian from Vamore arrived an hour ago during the trial," Torin said. "I thought you might be interested in meeting her."

Drocco slowed. "Where is she?"

"In the research room. She was eager to get started."

"Good," Drocco said. He had demoted the ruler of Vamore from king to duke, and since then the man had been reluctant to send any of his accomplished historians to Drocco's palace in Ashens. Drocco had been close to sending a small fleet to destroy Vamore and remind the Beta ruler that he resided in the Lox Empire now and could not refuse the emperor. Luckily the man had seen sense before it had been necessary. If the historian the duke sent was eager to help him push his investigation forward, that was even better. "I'll go and meet her first. Begin the preparations for the celebration."

Torin's brows rose. "You still want to have it?"

"Yes. It's not just for the army, it's also about solidifying the Lox Empire. I want the rulers of all of the cities and territories in attendance. They need to know the expectations of them if they are to keep their positions. I will decide later if the army will attend."

Torin nodded. "They should if you want to display your power."

Drocco grunted in agreement. "Make the preparations."

Torin stopped to bow and then turned back the way they came. Drocco watched him, a bubble of amusement bursting through his somber mood. That bow had been a salute only two short months ago. Now he was worthy of a bow. He turned and continued down the corridor.

The palace Drocco had inherited after destroying the King of Ashens was enormous. In fact, it was almost a small village, a ridiculous size for the king's family and small army. Drocco would have been surprised if they managed to fill even a quarter of it. However, it was clear it had been well built, with materials like marble, glass, and crystal being used in the king's private areas. The Lox filled it out nicely and it provided all necessary areas and rooms for them to settle comfortably.

A general air of peace drifted on the horizon for the Lox for the first time, and Drocco looked forward to it. He was finally in a position to address the vow he'd made to himself and his army—the one that had had every Alpha clamoring to be by his side—and now he had unlimited resources at his disposal to devote to it.

He turned down a series of corridors until he reached the library wing and then swung open the double doors to the main room where his research was stored.

Most of the books had been pulled from the shelves and stacked in short piles on multiple tables across the space and on the floor. Sheets of parchment seemed to be spread along every surface and balancing everywhere, while the folders that had held them were open in various areas of the room.

Drocco pinpointed the woman hunched over a desk in the far corner, peering at a sheet of parchment through handheld glass frames while bouncing tendrils of her hair dangled over the desk.

He maneuvered through the mess of the room to where she was, becoming increasingly annoyed that she hadn't addressed him when he entered. She didn't even straighten as he approached—surely she couldn't be that absorbed in her work.

"Found something worth sharing?" he asked, breaking the silence.

"When I need something, I'll let you know," she said, in an efficient tone tinged with annoyance. "That will be all."

A shot of irritation flared through Drocco. "I didn't realize historians had the authority to dismiss me."

The woman's head shot up, her face in a scowl until she saw who stood before her. Her deep brown eyes widened and she immediately straightened and dropped her head, her hands clasped in front of her. "My apologies, your Imperial Majesty. I wasn't expecting you." On the small side for a Beta, she stood straight and confident, suggesting she had experience with statesmen or royals.

Drocco found himself slightly irritated. Although he appreciated her professionalism, it was rare that someone of her size remained unfazed by his. He was the largest Alpha known in the Eastern Lands, and while it was a petty reaction for him to have, he found it bothered something innate within him. "This is my investigation; you will be working directly with me."

The woman's head rose slowly, confusion in her eyes. "Working... with you? Oh... I-I thought—"

Drocco looked her over as she cast around for something to say. Her dark brown eyes swept the room, avoiding him, and her curly copper-brown hair seemed to sway on its own with hardly any encouragement. Her features were pleasing—petite and well portioned—in fact, she was extremely attractive, even though no one thing about her stood out as being remarkable.

"I assumed you would be too busy to actually conduct the investigation yourself, your Imperial Majesty," she said, finally.

"You think there is anything more important right now than finding out what has happened to all the Omegas?" Drocco asked, almost mockingly. Everyone knew of the phenomenon and no one could explain it.

"I don't presume to know what is important to you," the Beta woman commented, somewhat dryly. "I'm just here to do a job."

Drocco's nostrils flared. "What?"

The woman's eyes widened and she lowered her head again. "I cannot assume what is important to you, your Imperial Majesty. I was only sent here to confirm and order your research."

Drocco stared at her. She had most certainly spoken out of turn. And yet, when asked to clarify her statement, she had simply repeated it. Choosing to let it slide, for now, he gestured to the piles of books and stacks of parchment. "Is there a reason for this mess? Have you found something?"

"Many of your records are out of order, your Imperial Majesty. I'm trying to sort them so that they make sense chronologically."

"That isn't much progress. I could get an administrator in here to do that."

"Yes, you could have," the woman said, in a low voice. "It would have made things easier for me."

Drocco's eyes narrowed, though with her head bowed, she couldn't see his face. "What is your name?" he asked.

"Miss Cailyn Lefroy."

She was unbonded. A satisfaction mellowed in him at the thought. Drocco frowned at the feeling and cast it aside. Why the hell did that matter? "Did you find that your rude and disrespectful attitude earned you favors in Vamore?"

The woman rose her head again, her eyes wide. "No... I apologize if I have displayed such an attitude, your Imperial Majesty. I'm known for my honesty and sometimes it can come across as being... I thought you would appreciate honesty."

Drocco said nothing. In truth, he would prefer honesty in all situations, but only wanted boldness from his warriors. Everyone else should be submissive to him and it was his right to expect that. "Honesty and rudeness are not mutually exclusive. Find the balance."

She frowned, and an urge to grab her neck came over him, but then her brows smoothed and her head dropped again. "I offer my apologies, your Imperial—"

"Emperor," he interrupted, annoyed with the long and awkward address. "Call me Emperor."

"Emperor," she whispered.

A slither of pleasure shuddered through him at the sound of her voice so quiet and intimate. He stilled, unfamiliar with the feeling. Something about her voice affected him. He watched her closely, looking at her stance and manner. She was a normal Beta, a little too bold, but nothing remarkable. He fucked plenty of Beta women but none of them had caused any kind of desire without more provocation than a tone of voice. Maybe he was due to get under one—it had been at least a week since he last had a woman in his bed.

He gazed at the historian for a moment longer and then moved away, back into the center of the room. "Tell me what you know."

The Beta lifted her head. "It has been at least one hundred and eleven years since Omegas began disappearing. First, all the adult Omegas in this city, Ashens, and then all surrounding cities and territories. The Western Lands reported the same about half a year after. The last publicly known siting of an Omega was on the White Ocean, and it is said she drowned.

"Then female children began disappearing— young children under the age of twelve before their dynamic could be discovered. Currently, female children are still disappearing soon after birth. It is assumed that all missing females are Omegas who have not yet been declared as such. Although many precautions are taken, it's impossible to predict which child may be targeted since their dynamic is not known."

Drocco turned toward the woman and watched her. She relaxed as she spoke, getting into her stride. The collared, tawny tunic that skimmed her curves was typical of Vamore wear but it didn't show enough of her natural shape for Drocco's liking.

"Children are still being taken all over the known Lands but with the prolonged lack of available Omegas, the Omega and Alpha birth rates are beginning to decline. Most Alphas born over the last few decades have been to Beta parents and they only come from Betas who have Alphas in their immediate family."

"I don't need to know about the effects of this on the Lands," Drocco interjected. He was highly sensitive to the fact that Alphas could eventually become endangered if the current situation continued, but he refused to discuss it with anyone. "I want to know how to find them or stop them from being taken."

"From what I have gathered, it is almost impossible to stop the Omega children being taken. There are mishaps and coincidences that cause no one to be around when they disappear. Many claim the use of the Talent is the reason—reports suggest that bodyguards lose their memories and locked rooms remained undisturbed, however, there is no concrete proof of this. It is possible, and likely, that all of the Omegas are still alive, although whether they are in good health cannot be known."

Drocco's attention peaked. "How do you know they're alive?"

"There is nothing to suggest they are killed when they are taken or that they are killed at all," the historian said, moving around the corner desk to a stack of parchment on a smaller desk next to it. "The late King of Ashens made agreements with all territories that exist in the Eastern, Western, and Southern Lands. Every city was searched peacefully and no bodies were ever found. There was also a sighting of a carriage filled with Omegas heading toward Neka twenty years ago. At the time, the witness thought herself mistaken but soon after, Beta males in the area claimed they could smell that Omegas had been there."

"Why was this never made public?" Drocco asked.

"The ruler of Neka didn't want to be accused of harboring Omegas and have his territory turned upside down by numerous rulers on the say-so of a few unreliable witnesses. So he suppressed the information."

"Neka is now part of the Lox Empire," Drocco said, his voice low. "He will have to answer to me."

"That ruler died five years ago," the woman said. "He was succeeded by his daughter."

"It makes no difference," Drocco said, dismissively. "She accepted his title so she must accept his mistakes."

The historian said nothing. She stood by the smaller desk, a wad of parchment in her hands.

"Continue," Drocco ordered.

"That is all I can say for certain right now, your Imp— Emperor."

Drocco nodded. She seemed to already know more detail than he did. "You will work in this room and liaise only with me on this. Nothing is to be copied or taken from this room. Understood?"

The woman hesitated. "May I ask why, Emperor? It's just that many of the records are decaying and if they were copied—"

"This information has been collected over the last eighty years starting from my grandfather's time. It holds witness accounts, detailed descriptions, statistics and information that can no longer be readily found. It shall not leave this room. If you have a concern about a record becoming destroyed, you speak to me."

The woman nodded. "Understood."

"How long will it take you to compile all of this information?"

"Will I get any assistance?"

"No."

She pressed her lips together, surveying the room. "Three months."

"That's too long," Drocco growled.

"Then I need assistance. At least three administrators should lessen the workload and bring it down to one month."

"You are aware that this information is highly sought after?" Drocco said. "I cannot allow it to fall into the hands of those that would make more significant progress than me."

The woman's eyes narrowed. "Is this a competition for you?"

"It is a challenge," Drocco said, sharply. "One that everyone else has failed."

"You have already united the Eastern Lands under one name, how many challenges do you need to accomplish in your lifetime to feel complete?"

"Every single one that presents itself to me," Drocco snapped.

The woman ground her jaw together, her eyes flashing. "Then give me three months. The Omegas have already been missing for over one hundred years. What is three months?"

A sudden shock hit Drocco like a pail of ice cold water. She was *arguing* with him. And what was more astonishing was that he hadn't even noticed at first.

He moved to her in a flash, whipping up sheets of parchment in his wake. Planting himself in front of her, he trapped her against the desk, as parchment floated down around them. "You seem to have a problem understanding your place," he said between gritted teeth. A hot annoyance buzzed within him accompanied by something he couldn't quite identify.

She began to lower her head, but he grabbed her neck and forced her head up. "Oh no you don't," he murmured. "Do not try to adopt a meek stance now. You are one of those Betas who think you already rule the world but I can assure you, Betas will never get to that stage. I will find the Omegas we deserve, and a whole generation of Alphas will be born."

She stared up at him with those bright eyes and he rubbed his hand over the smooth skin of her neck and lower jaw, so small he could easily crush it with a sharp squeeze. Her honey-colored skin felt like velvet and he found himself staring at it, a thrum of desire skipping through him. It had definitely been too long since he'd had a woman.

"You seem to be a challenge all of your own," he mused. "You have an unruly manner, even for a Beta. I'm surprised you have been allowed this position."

"I'm the best there is," she said, her voice strained.

He realized he held her too tight, but squeezed her neck tighter before releasing her. She gasped for breath but didn't lower her head.

Something about her was intriguing. Drocco looked into her eyes for any signs of submission, any hint of why he might be attracted to her, but there was none. He leaned into her, then frowned. Her scent was disappointingly bland. Still, part of him wanted to have her imprisoned and tortured, while the other part ached to bend her over and fuck her right there. All of him wanted to dominate her; have her recognize him as Alpha and submit accordingly. But any time he forced a Beta to submit as an Omega naturally would, it rendered them mostly useless for anything else. He couldn't make use of her skills on the investigation if she was begging for his cock every hour.

"You will have your three months," he said.

She took a shaky breath and nodded, finally lowering her head.

He turned and left the room. Those three months were for him as much as for her. He would enjoy her beauty, her skills, and her defiance and then make her pay for each and every indiscretion when the investigation ended. He smiled, thinking of her snappy retorts, her pretty mouth, and all that curly hair. It would be worth it.

CHAPTER TWO

CAILYN

As soon as the emperor left, Cailyn let out a heavy breath of relief. She fell against the desk trembling, bracing herself with both hands and breathing deeply. What the fuck was that? It was almost as if he could tell she was an Omega.

Steadying herself, she made her way back to the desk in the corner and sat down. Closing her eyes, she focused her mind and checked her magical blocks from the top of her head through her entire body to the soles of her feet. All were securely in place.

She opened her eyes, biting her lip in thought. The emperor's behavior had made her think at least one of her blocks had been knocked askew. He glared at her with those cold black eyes as though he knew she hid something, and when he grabbed her, he rubbed her neck like he wanted to force her to submit. The crazy thing was, she almost did. She almost went limp as soon as his massive, rough hand closed around her neck and jaw, and she'd had to fight against the automatic reaction. She shouldn't have had that response—that was the whole point of the fucking blocks.

She sighed and rubbed her forehead. The emperor was much more terrifying than she'd imagined. Massive, bulky, and animalistic, he was so Alpha he was almost a ridiculous stereotype. His wild black hair, the way he prowled the room, his arrogance and demands—all typical of an Alpha with no limit to his ego. The only thing that had surprised her was his way of communicating. Most Alphas she had come across were unable to articulate themselves so well, even if they were smart. They lacked the patience to reason with anyone. The emperor had shown great patience with her rebellious comments and she had expected punishment when she kept pushing. She hadn't been able to help it. With her Omega instincts blocked, it was easy to be as pushy and sarcastic as she wanted, and it was difficult not to be when she utterly despised him. He represented every reason why Omegas would never return to normal society. The fact he thought he deserved them, like they were property to be owned, was enough of a reason to fuck up his investigation.

Tapping her fingers on the desk, Cailyn surveyed the room but did not see any of it. Now she had met him, she could properly form a plan. Firstly, her reaction to him needed to be corrected. He had to have been emitting Alpha pheromones, and if she hadn't been blocked, her superior Omega sense of smell would have been overwhelmed and she would have ended up at his feet in a pool of slick begging him to fill her. She shouldn't have been physically affected by him at all and couldn't afford for that to happen again. She was the most accomplished Omega in the compound with the Talent, which was the reason why she was given the mission in the first place. Since she didn't have any contact with the Mothers to ask them why this had happened, the best she could do was reinforce her blocks and try to stay away from him.

Secondly, the investigation. It was well known that Emperor Drocco had been collecting information for decades, and now that he secured the Eastern Lands and was restructuring it as the Lox Empire, the Mothers wanted to make sure he would not find the Omega Compound. She had been sent to find out how much he knew about the Omegas and mislead him. However, if he wasn't going to allow her to copy or remove any information, and if he was going to be working closely with her, it would be difficult to secure anything pertinent. She would need to commit important things to memory or use the Talent.

She stood, finally looking carefully at the room. The three-month time frame she had told the emperor wasn't entirely accurate. She really only required one and a half to two months, but she needed the breathing space. She had intercepted the real Miss Camille Lefroy only that morning, taken her identity, and had her hidden. Although she had studied her for months, many things could go wrong if anyone was to suspect she wasn't who she said she was. Luckily the real Miss Lefroy only went by her family name in her profession, and her friends and family called her Cece; very few people knew her real name. Still, one letter from Vamore would be all it would take to impede her mission or cause her immediate death. She needed to be careful.

She firmed her mind and got to work with new enthusiasm, sorting and reading the books and files. The quicker she got this done, the quicker she could leave this mission and Emperor Drocco behind.

***

For the next week, the emperor came to see her three times a day. He arrived at the research room every morning, midday, and late afternoon to find out what she had discovered. He made her tell him everything she had found during her reading and then forced her to theorize an opinion. Of course, her opinion kept changing the more she unearthed, and she was feeling mentally exhausted with the constant analyzing.

At the beginning of the second week, she returned to her private quarters at midday to avoid him. Her quarters were not far from the research room and consisted of a beautifully furnished living area with an entire wall of glass that looked out over Ashens city, a spacious bedroom, bathroom, and kitchen area. Lying on her bed, reading a letter from the real Miss Lefroy's sister, she fell asleep.

A strange air around her caused her to stir awake. She blinked, suddenly alert, and slowly sat up. Turning to glance around her quarters, she screamed in shock. Emperor Drocco loomed next to her bed, his wide build blocking almost all the light.

"Emperor," she gasped. "What are you doing in here?"

"This is my palace," he said, gruffly. "I can go anywhere I choose."

She bit her tongue to avoid responding with an angry retort. She valued her privacy, especially with her occupation. Taking a breath to calm her racing heart, she secured herself upright, keeping her eyes low. "How can I help you, Emperor?"

"You know I am due to see you at midday," he said. "I arrived today and you weren't there."

"I wasn't aware I was required to be there."

"Of course you are," he barked. "I need an update and an analysis."

She lifted her eyes to meet his. "These updates are causing me mental fatigue, Emperor. They also waste a lot of time. In a week, I have done a fifth of the work possible because I keep being interrupted to stop and explain things to you."

The emperor's eyes narrowed. "I need nothing *explained* to me. I have read every single one of those files," he said, his tone sharp. "I'm making sure you are as good as your reputation suggests."

Cailyn made a face. "If you don't trust my reputation, why have you allowed me on the investigation?"

"You are being interviewed." His eyes glittered from the shadows on his face. "And this midday nap does not bode well for your continued employment."

Cailyn's mood lifted. If he retired her from the investigation that would be perfect. She could simply take the useful information she had found so far and leave unscathed. "Are you bringing in another researcher?"

The emperor looked down at her for a long moment but she couldn't see his expression with the shadows across his face. That trembly feeling began to rise in her again and she tensed, hoping it wouldn't overwhelm her.

"Get back to the research room." He spun on his heel, his black robes twirling around his enormous frame, and left the room.

Cailyn's mood sunk as she fixed her hair and headed back to the research room. Maybe she had just made things worse for herself. He was probably offended that she had criticized him, but she wasted half an afternoon sleeping because of his ridiculous interrogations. He needed to know.

The emperor stood in the center of the research room talking to another man when she arrived—a man dressed in the rich red cape of the Lox and not the gray robe of a servant. However, he was slimmer than most of the Lox, with a head of curly brown hair and silver-gray eyes. Commander Torin. Cailyn had read about him. At one point in the past, she had considered accepting a mission to seduce him in order to get close to the Lox. He was the only Beta in the army and that alone made him interesting, but there was as little information about him as there was about the emperor. As she approached them, their conversation ended. Commander Torin walked past her without giving her a second glance.

"How are you organizing the records?" the emperor asked.

"I've created piles for each decade and spread them a little so files and other information can slip in," Cailyn explained. "Why?"

The emperor glanced down at her. "That isn't your usual method."

A sudden heat spread through Cailyn. He knew Miss Lefroy's methods. "I thought this way would work better considering the variety of subject matter."

The emperor made a noise in the back of his throat, before moving quickly around the room. "I think your usual method would work better."

Cailyn stood for a moment trying to think of which of Miss Lefroy's methods he referred to. When he began to pull the tables around the room, she knew which one. The Chron Line—the most popular method of organizing research that Miss Lefroy had developed.

Over the next few moments, Emperor Drocco pulled a number of tables to make a line across the length of the research room. He shot her a hard look any time she moved to help, so she just watched and injected where necessary. Next, they decided how to order the information chronologically down the table, with areas cordoned off for specialist information.

"This should make the research easier to organize," the emperor murmured, observing the new layout. "It is a good method."

Cailyn dipped her head in a nod. "Thank you. When will you be checking in next?"

The man walked around the tables slowly until he faced her. "I want your comments on all of the files you have examined," he said, his voice somewhat soft.

Cailyn kept her eyes locked on his, unable to lower them as he came closer. His dark eyes looked different than normal—shiny and luminous.

"I want to be able to see your opinions on the research."

Cailyn frowned. "You want my opinion permanently recorded on the files?"

"You are the most accomplished historian in the Eastern Lands aren't you? Why not?"

Cailyn lowered her head, that strange trembling feeling creeping over her again. He stood too close. "Yes, Emperor. Of course."

He stood silently in front of her and then lifted a hand to her chin, a rough brush against her skin as his finger lifted her eyes to his. "You have the job."

Cailyn nodded. "Thank you, Emperor."

As he stared at her, the feeling increased, expanding over every inch of her being. His hand twisted and began to close around her throat.

"Emperor, I really need to get started," she said, forcing her voice to stay calm. "Is there anything else?"

His hand slowed, brushed down her neck, and then moved away. "No," he said, his eyes running over her before turning and leaving the room.

The next morning, Cailyn asked the servant that took her lunch order for some extra parchment to be brought to the research room. If she had secured the job, the emperor would no longer be watching her closely and she could get on with her plans. With the spare parchment, she began to copy information she knew the Mothers would be interested in: sightings of Omegas that hadn't been recorded with them, an attempted collaboration between the Eastern and Western Lands to find them, the use of the Talent to try and locate them, and the progress made by the King of Ashens that had taken him dangerously close to the Omega Compound.

She spent most of the morning copying and adjusting the records and then reading some of the history of the Eastern Lands. She was so involved reading about the political structuring of the elusive Southern Lands, when she looked up, it was already past midmorning. She stood and stretched, then turned to sort the file into its place on the table.

The emperor sat staring at her from a corner of the room.

She stiffened, her heart jumping into her throat.

They stared at each other for a long moment. How long had he been sitting there?

"Can I help you, Emperor?" she asked hesitantly, as her heartbeat calmed.

"No," he answered.

She stared at him for a moment, unsure why he sat in the room. Surely he had come to speak to her? What had he seen and how long had he been sitting there? Did he suspect her?

"You may continue with your work," the emperor said after she'd been standing there for a while, his voice a deep rumble throughout the room.

Cailyn looked at the file in her hand, flustered. She'd forgotten what she had intended to do with it. After rereading it, she sorted it into its correct place on the tables and went back to the pile she had assigned herself for the day. She glanced at the emperor and he still watched her.

For the rest of the morning, he remained in the corner, a silent, motionless, massive bulk watching her every move. Cailyn ignored him as best as she could but by midday, a frustration had built up. How was she going to continue with her real work if she was being watched so closely? This was worse than him visiting her every quarter hour. Didn't he have anything else to do?

She brushed off her hands and left the room, heading to her quarters. She needed to think without the presence of the emperor, and she needed to eat.

Cailyn sat on a low, wide chair in the living room staring out over the city, munching the thick beef and cheese sandwich that had been laid out for her. At the rate she was going, it would take about a week to get the research room into any kind of logical order. So far, she had seen all kinds of random information; from the line of successors in each territory in the Western Lands to the various traditions and cultures seen in one city throughout the years. The emperor surely liked to collect knowledge, even if he just dumped it in a room for someone else to sort out.

"This is what you asked for, for lunch?"

Cailyn jumped, her curse caught behind a chunk of bread in her throat. She spun around to see the emperor peering down at her plate.

Coughing and spluttering, she moved away from him to spit out the food.

"This is not a suitable meal." The emperor peered at her plate disapprovingly. "No wonder you are small for a Beta."

A slight fear gripped Cailyn as she tried to compose herself. She was small for a Beta because she wasn't a Beta.

"You don't need to eat frugally while you're staying here," he said. "I will ensure your lunch is adequate from now on."

"This is my private quarters, Emperor," she said sharply, her throat raw. "Why do you keep entering uninvited?"

"You left the research room," he said, nonchalantly. "I came to see where you'd gotten to."

"Am I supposed to clear my every movement with you?" she said, her voice tinged with disgust.

His gaze intensified. "Would that be a problem for you? I'm your employer."

"I need a certain level of independence to do my work, Emperor," Cailyn said, her annoyance creeping into her tone. "I know that's not something you value, but in order to get the best out of—"

"What do you mean by that?" His eyes narrowed.

"I mean, I understand that you want everyone to be subservient to you but some of us are completely capable of doing a good job without constant monitoring."

"This investigation is important to me and I will not leave it in the hands of someone who has come from Vamore, possibly with a hatred toward the Lox and their own agenda," he said. "You can dislike it as much as you want, but it will not change. I want to know where you are at all times."

Cailyn glared at him, but couldn't argue with his logic. He wouldn't know if Miss Lefroy was loyal to the Lox or not. She should have thought about that more carefully, and she would have—if she'd known she'd be working directly with him.

"And yes, I do expect everyone to be subservient to me," he added, moving around the couch between them. "I'm the most accomplished Alpha in every Land that exists. Expecting subservient behavior is my right."

"Just like it's your right to have an Omega?" Cailyn snapped, her annoyance breaking down all self-preserving cautions she had given herself to be polite to him. Fuck him. This man had an ego the size of the entire Eastern Lands. "Whether she wants it or not?"

"Of course it is my right. It is the right of all Alphas to have their Omegas. It is the only way to live a life that is complete," he said calmly, stepping toward her. "I don't expect any Beta to understand it. You don't have that kind of connection—that kind of want or need that an Alpha has for an Omega. You have not been blessed with that and you shouldn't try to understand something you will never experience. As for what my Omega wants?"

He came closer still, and Cailyn backed away. She couldn't have him close to her again.

"Any Omega would find it an honor to be with me," he said, a determined gleam in his eyes. "Only I can provide her with what she needs and craves. It is an absolute atrocity that these abductors have kept Omegas away from the men that could give them that gift."

Cailyn pressed her lips shut. Anything she said right now would reveal too much about what she knew about Omegas. His traditionalist views were so archaic, it was almost humorous, but what did she expect? Everything he had learned about Omegas was from the Alphas of times past. And they had been animals.

"In fact," he added. "It is akin to torture."

"Torture?" Cailyn scoffed before she even thought about it. "It is torture to *not* be fucked and dominated into some kind of slave by some massive, egotistical Alpha?"

Her laugh had barely left her before the emperor rushed toward her in a flash and slammed her up against the wall behind her. She gasped in shock and blinked, looking into his stormy eyes, her fear rising. She had gone too far in provoking him and who knew what he might do now? But as she continued staring, she realized no anger clouded his gaze. Annoyance, yes. Conviction, yes. Even a tinge of curiosity. But no anger. She held her relief in her throat, trying not to breathe in his scent. Even though she couldn't really smell it, she knew it was there because that trembly feeling cut through all others as a signal, a beacon directly to him.

He leaned into her ear. "Do not mock things you have no understanding of, kitten," he whispered. "You have barely left the luxuries of your life in Vamore, surrounded by old books and statues, to even brace the concept of torture or need." She shivered as he leaned into her and ran his nose up her neck, breathing her in. "But you will."

He let her go and she slumped against the table next to her trying to process what he had said. Had he just threatened her?

"Finish your pitiful lunch and get back to the research room," he ordered.

As he walked away, Cailyn drew herself upright trying to hide her shaking. She should have abandoned this mission when she first realized he would be her contact. For some reason, this man affected her in a way no other Alpha did. She found it difficult to hold her tongue around him and at the same time wanted to submit so desperately when he stood close. She had ignored the potential threat in favor of getting the knowledge the Mothers needed, but he knew much more about the real Miss Lefroy than she had anticipated. One wrong move and she could be discovered. She had to work quickly and carefully, and get the fuck out of the palace.

CHAPTER THREE

DROCCO

The historian was becoming a severe distraction.

Drocco was unsure exactly what it was, but something about her aroused and intrigued him, sparking a fierce need to dominate her. It was a strange feeling—one he'd never had before. He sat in the corner of the research room watching her daily for nearly a month trying to figure it out. It couldn't be her smart mouth—he most definitely preferred submissive types, even in Betas. Her bland scent wasn't enticing, so it couldn't be that. It couldn't be her dynamic since he was looking for his Omega. Betas were sufficient to slake his needs, but the pleasures an Omega could give were known to be incomparable. It could be the historian's looks. It would seem as though a studious woman in shapeless clothing with brown hair and eyes would be easily forgettable, but it was quite the opposite. She was uniquely attractive in a way he found slightly fascinating. Yes, that had to be it. She was beautiful and he wanted a taste of her, yet was forced to wait. That must be what caused this unhealthy draw to her. He'd never had to wait to fuck anyone before.

After meeting her that first time, he had summoned a Beta female known for her talented mouth to relieve him of his arousal, but as she knelt to tend to him, he lost interest. She had been stunned when he ordered her away and, in truth, he had surprised himself; however, he'd been reeling from the historian's bluntly antagonistic comments and he couldn't focus on gratification. He spent the rest of the evening looking over the profile of her that they had obtained when they had learned she was coming. It suggested nothing of her personal life or personality—it just contained dry, factual information about her impressive abilities and skills as a historian.

As Drocco continued to watch her, he noticed little things about her manner. When she read something she found interesting, she played with her right earlobe. She pursed her full lips when she read something she didn't quite like and bit her bottom lip when she was trying to decide where something should go on the Chron Line. The way she moved around the room was sexy as hell, smooth and fluid, very feline, and when she knelt on the floor sorting random files, her rich copper curls bouncing over them, he had to grip the arms of his chair to stop himself heading over there, pinning her to the ground and ripping away her clothes. The simplest thing would be to stay away from her completely, but when he wasn't in the room, he thought about her constantly. He hated it. He was always in control of everything and this impulse was too wild. He couldn't wait for the day the investigation ended so he could claim what he wanted and move on.

"Your Imperial Majesty," came a soft voice from beside him.

He turned to see a servant standing by the door.

The man grimaced. "You have a visitor."

"Who?" His gaze returned to Cailyn.

"Commander Torin, your Imperial Majesty."

Drocco nodded, rose from his chair, and headed outside. He had told the guard at the door that he didn't want anyone entering unannounced. He hadn't liked the way Cailyn had looked at Torin when he had last been in the room. They were both Betas and Torin was possibly the most accomplished Beta male in Ashens—a great prospect for any Beta female— but the idea Cailyn might find him attractive irritated Drocco beyond all reason.

"Drocco," Torin greeted. "Good morning."

Drocco returned the greeting.

"You have instructed that no one enter?" Torin asked somewhat incredulously, gesturing to the research room. Drocco had never refused him entry to any area of the palace.

"I don't want Miss Lefroy interrupted," Drocco said, briskly. "What is it?"

Torin's eyes swept over him. "You have been very focused on this investigation, Drocco."

"That is the intention, Torin," Drocco said lightly. "I made a vow and I'm trying to keep it."

"How is it going?"

"Well so far," Drocco said. "Miss Lefroy is ordering the information and highlighting key points to focus on. I've sent scouts to a couple of cities to look into a number of loose ends. I trust you have made contact with the ruler of Neka?"

Torin nodded. "Yes, I am dealing with it. I'm glad it is going well. We've had communication from Eiros."

Drocco's mood darkened. "And?"

"Malloron would like to meet."

"When?"

"In two days. He has suggested a portal."

"He is not entering my Empire through a portal," Drocco said, his voice low.

"No, he wishes to talk through it," Torin explained. "To use it as a method of communicating."

Drocco lifted his head in understanding. He needed to speak to Malloron and make his own position clear, as the ruler of Lox Empire, but the distance between them meant their communication was always prolonged. Eiros was situated in the Western Lands, which was across the White Ocean, and it took months for messages to pass between them. If they could talk face to face it would secure things much more quickly.

"He is very keen to meet via this method and has insisted that nothing untoward will come of it," Torin said, after a few long moments of silence.

"Your thoughts?" Drocco asked.

"I think it will be good to face him directly, as I'm sure you realize," Torin said. "You are very persuasive in person."

"If he can create a portal here to communicate, he can create a portal at any time to use as a doorway," Drocco said, an edge in his voice at the idea.

"Yes," Torin admitted. "That is a possibility."

Drocco exhaled harshly. "This is why I want the use of the Talent disabled as soon as possible, Torin!"

"If we are to make significant headway protecting ourselves from the Talent, this opportunity to analyze a portal would be of great benefit."

"Hmm…" Drocco let out a throaty grumble.

"If he truly can create a doorway here, he will do so if he wishes, whether we agree to the meet or not," Torin pointed out. "At least if you agree, we will have a time and place to focus our attention to learn more about the Talent."

That was true. "All right," Drocco said. "Set it up."

Torin nodded. "He said he will make an attempt in two days, so I will ensure we are ready to receive him." He glanced at the research room. "Is this where you can be found now?"

"Yes," Drocco replied. "But I only want to be interrupted if it's absolutely necessary."

"Understood." With that, Torin bowed and headed down the corridor.

When Drocco entered the research room, he automatically swept the room for Cailyn. She stood in one corner, her head tilted, her lips pursed and a frown on her face.

"What is it?" he asked.

"These records have big gaps," she murmured, almost to herself.

"What are they?"

"Records of the Omega population before they went missing."

Drocco crossed the room to her. "That is important. How do you know there are gaps?"

"The King of Ashens had a count completed when he first came into power. It totaled over one hundred and twenty-five thousand. There were only seven thousand in the most recent count. That's too low. There's data missing."

Drocco looked at the files, leaning into her to breathe in her scent. Even though it was bland, he took every opportunity to experience it—another strange behavior he didn't understand. He pushed the thought away and focused on the topic at hand. They needed accurate figures of the number of Omegas at all times. "How many counts did the king do?"

"I've only found two so far."

Drocco nodded. "Tomorrow we will go to the Records Keep and find out the accurate number."

Cailyn blinked at him. "The Records Keep?"

"Yes, in Ashens. They keep all important records for the Eastern Lands," Drocco said, settling into his chair. "It's one of the reasons why Ashens is the most influential territory in the East. I have yet to visit it but I knew my investigations would take me there eventually." He frowned. "I'm sure you would've been there before."

"A few times yes." She stood thinking for a moment. "I don't mind going on my own if you have things to do."

"We will go at midday," Drocco said, ending the conversation.

Cailyn nodded slowly before going back to her work.

❖

In the carriage on the way to the Records Keep, Cailyn was restless. She wouldn't look at him, barely spoke to him, and subtly fidgeted in the seat opposite. Drocco simply watched her. She was like a pet that needed to be soothed. She had snapped at him the previous afternoon and seemed to have a looser hold on her tongue since he entered the research room that morning. Something about the trip was making her apprehensive, but he couldn't figure out what. After watching her for a few moments, he stopped caring. Her curly hair was up today, exposing her slim neck and showing off her neckline and shoulders. Every time she moved he wanted to bite every inch of exposed flesh, suck on her, lick her... a thrill went through him at the thought of her response—the breathy sounds she would utter, her moans and whispers. As his eyes traveled down her body, stopping at every curve he could almost see that he wanted to explore; he noticed her knees were pressed tightly together. He glanced up at her but she was staring fixedly out of the carriage window. He suppressed a dark smile.

The Records Keep stood in the center of Ashens. Tall and cream-colored, with elegant swirls engraved into its walls, it was surrounded by equally sophisticated buildings important to the running of Ashens, but not all of them had survived the Lox invasion as well as the Records Keep. It seemed the King of Ashens had been particularly precious about making his city look bland and boring. Drocco found the broken jagged buildings that had suffered the effects of battle to be more interesting. Redesigning his Empire to look strong and powerful was something he looked forward to.

A number of emerald-robed record keepers nervously greeted him and his traveling party, all gathered at the entrance of the Keep at his arrival.

"Greetings, your Imperial Majesty," each of them murmured as they bowed low. They all seemed to look the same with pale skin and blond hair, and all were Betas.

One of them rose first, an older man with slanted eyes and a neat, gray beard. "I am Head Keeper Galan," he said. "We are honored to have you visit, Emperor. Would you like a tour of the Keep?"

"No," Drocco said. "I want a guide."

"I would be happy to assist you with anything you need, your Imperial Majesty," the keeper said, bowing again.

"I want the records on the population count of the Eastern Lands over the last four hundred years."

The keeper nodded. He led them through the quiet building, up a few flights of stairs, and along a number of slim corridors. Bookshelves and filing cabinets made up most of the interior with a number of windows punctuated throughout to let in natural light. They passed a number of gray-robed clerks filing large piles of parchment or scribbling intensely on desks tucked away in slightly obscured corners. A peaceful silence swamped the building that made even their muffled footsteps on the carpet seem too loud. Finally, the keeper arrived at a long room with windows along one wall and floor-to-ceiling shelves on the other.

"All population count results are kept here," the keeper said. "We knew that you might soon be interested in information about Omegas, so we cataloged some information specifically for you, your Imperial Majesty."

"Information like what?" Drocco asked, his interest peaked.

"Mainly information about birth rates of different dynamics, jobs Omegas tended to thrive in, the number of bonded partners, rare dynamic variants, that kind of thing."

"Do you have that information readily available?"

The head keeper nodded. "Of course, follow me."

"I'll stay and look at these documents, if that's all right, Emperor?" Cailyn interjected.

He nodded. "Compare them to my data." He signaled to his guards to stay with Cailyn and followed the head keeper.

As they climbed the stairs a few floors, the head keeper explained how the Records Keep worked. The previous four Kings of Ashens hired clerks who spread far and wide into the Eastern Lands and, over the years, recorded their observations in an objective, methodical manner. Sometimes they were given specific information to collect, other times they were told to explore or investigate, while others recorded things by chance, but all were sent back to the Records Keep for filing and recording. The recently deceased King of Ashens made a point of always keeping up-to-date with all of the records, and that was how he became the most powerful ruler in the Eastern Lands—he simply knew more than most of the other territories combined and could choose to interfere in ways they didn't understand.

Drocco found it illuminating. He listened carefully, interjecting questions where necessary to form a complete picture of the value of the Records Keep. He had been keeping his records in a muddled mess of information, but the King of Ashens had turned it into a weapon. And without spilling blood. For the first time, he felt a glimmer of admiration toward the Beta king. Even though the man had made many unwise choices, his use of this facility was not one of them.

As he spoke, the head keeper led Drocco upstairs until he was out of breath and then walked across an entire floor to regain his strength. When they reached the stairs on the other side, the keeper continued his ascent. This pattern repeated until they arrived on the top floor.

"This is the floor we have been arranging just for you, your Imperial Majesty," the head keeper said, wheezing a little. "It has every piece of information that pertains to Omegas since the first disappearance. We are still copying files but within the next month or so it should be complete. You are welcome to visit anytime to peruse at your leisure or with the guidance of a keeper." The keeper's hands twitched and he glanced around the room. "Of course, if you prefer to dismantle the Records Keep we can assist with storage or—"

"I will not be dismantling this facility," Drocco confirmed. This was one of the most impressive things he had ever seen in the Eastern Lands so far, and he finally understood why many held it in such high esteem. He would definitely not be getting rid of it.

The keeper seemed to let out a sigh of relief. "Thank you, your Imperial Majesty. We wondered what may become of everything here; it would be a shame for such information to be lost." He paused, looking around the room. "Would you like to browse anything while you're here?"

For the next hour, Drocco looked at the factual data around birth rates. It was as bad as he had imagined. Over the decades, Alphas birth rates were in steady decline since the Omegas disappearance. This trend was true in every territory and there was even data from the Western Lands showing the same.

Drocco left the floor in a somber mood but was impressed by the quality of data collected about the Western Lands. Clearly, the King of Ashens had sent clerks over there too. He questioned the head keeper about this at length and resolved to talk to Torin about it. If Malloron had the gall to send spies to Drocco, it wouldn't hurt to send a fleet to pressure him in his own territory.

He headed back down to the population room, and as he crossed the floor he froze at the sight that greeted him. Cailyn stood laughing and talking to a clerk just outside the room—a Beta male clerk who stood too close to her and looked at her in a way that suggested he was very familiar with her.

A rush of darkness embraced Drocco, and he was moving toward them before he could even register it.

As he neared, Cailyn's brown eyes widened, the smile dropping from her face, while the Beta shrank back.

"What the fuck are you doing?" Drocco bellowed. "Is this your job? Standing around socializing like you haven't a thought in your head?" His voice rose to almost a roar and seemed to bound off every surface in the quiet building.

Cailyn opened her mouth but nothing came out.

He turned to advance on the Beta, his body moving almost without control. "Run" was all the warning he could get out.

As the Beta escaped, Cailyn found her voice. Although it shook, it stopped him in his tracks. "I finished looking at the population data. I was waiting for you to—"

"Do not test me, Cailyn Lefroy," Drocco said in a hoarse, low voice, stalking toward her. "I leave you for a short moment and you're talking in a very friendly manner to a member of staff who is no doubt still loyal to the King of Ashens."

Cailyn backed away into the room, her eyes fiery as she looked up at him. "You have been gone close to two hours, Emperor."

"That does not explain your behavior!" Drocco barked, forcing her back until she reached the wall. "When we are out of the palace, I expect you to behave as though you are—"

He bit off the word about to come out of his mouth, a sudden shock dampening his rage.

Mine.

No. That's not what he had intended to say... was it?

He floundered, searching for words. "—capable of common sense," he finished. "If you cannot do that, you are inappropriately skilled to do anything on this investigation that is of use to me."

Cailyn was silent for a long moment. "I would like to resign my post, Emperor."

Drocco's jaw slacked. "What?"

"I don't think I'm right for your investigation. I think you could find a more suitable historian for your needs."

Drocco laughed, low and hard. "Do you think you are still in Vamore?" He planted his wide hands on either side of her head and leaned down. "Or Neka, or Grence? Do you think you're even in Ashens? You are in the Lox Empire, kitten. And your employment doesn't end until I fucking end it."

Cailyn stared at him steadily, her eyes hard, no fear or shock present, and something fierce bloomed in Drocco's chest. He glanced at her perfect mouth, a raw desperation rising to take it—fuck waiting.

"The Omegas were dying," she said, bitterly.

Drocco frowned at the sudden change in topic. "What?"

"The Omegas were dying at unnatural rates before their disappearance." She ducked under his arm and headed to a pile she had collated on the floor. Drocco exhaled harshly, pushing away the anger that had almost risen to an acute peak. Or was that desire? He approached Cailyn's pile stack wearily. This woman loved her piles of parchment.

"The data in these files match the data we have," she said, shoving a stack into Drocco's hands. "There was a serious decline in Omegas from the first count

43

to the last. There were too many deaths for it to be a natural occurrence."

Drocco stood gripping the files for a long moment. This, he had never heard before. Omegas had been dying? That couldn't be possible. It hadn't ever been reported.

"Head Keeper!" he called.

Within seconds the head keeper appeared at the door of the room. "How can I help you, Emperor?"

"Explain why Omegas were dying."

The man clasped his hands in front of him as he headed into the room. "I'm afraid that is something we do not have data on."

"Why the fuck not?"

"No one reported or recorded any information on it, your Imperial Majesty," he responded, his voice trembling. "Please remember, the data gathered is most comprehensive from when the late king's family came into power. Before that, there was no culture of recording events or occurrences. We have noticed the declining numbers of Omegas but we cannot explain it with factual information."

"What theory would you surmise based on the information you do have?" Cailyn asked.

The head keeper hesitated. "We don't like to theorize—"

"Answer," Drocco ordered.

The head keeper swallowed. "It's possible the Omegas were under some kind of attack," he said, carefully. "But we cannot guess what kind of attack and we do not recommend you take that theory seriously, your Imperial Majesty."

A short moment of silence expanded in the room as Drocco digested the information. If Omegas were under attack, it had to be by Betas. They were the most numerous dynamic and had much to gain by killing Omegas and thereby reducing the birth rates of Alphas. Before he could think it through properly, Cailyn headed to the door.

"Where are you going?" Drocco said sharply.

"We're finished here, aren't we?" she snapped, her eyes flashing at him.

The head keeper blanched as she stormed past him while Drocco watched her. Her anger was causing her to be carelessly willful and surprisingly entertaining, despite the rudeness.

He inclined his head at his guards at the door and they blocked her path. She tried to push past them and they grabbed her, holding onto her arms until she stilled. A dust of rage skimmed over Drocco at the sight of their hands on her, but he forced himself to ignore it. She was causing the restraint to be necessary.

"I'll be back to look into the documents you have selected for me in more detail, Head Keeper," he told the man as he turned to go. "I will also consider how your facility may be of full use to the Lox Empire. In the meantime, notify Lox Palace if you or your keepers or clerks find anything that you think would be of use to me."

The head keeper bowed deeply. "I shall, your Imperial Majesty. We look forward to your next visit."

As he passed the guards, Drocco served Cailyn with a fierce look, heavy with all the rage rocketing within him. She immediately relaxed into a submissive pose, and a gleam of satisfaction pierced through him at her reaction. Yes, he would enjoy training this one.

"You will walk, unaided, to my carriage," he said, harshly. "And you will get yourself under control. It is your choice whether you continue working on this investigation with all of your limbs intact. Understood?"

Cailyn nodded, her head low, in the correct position, yet Drocco was momentarily annoyed he couldn't see her face.

"Good. Let her go."

On the return journey, Cailyn kept quiet. She sat with her head down and her hands in her lap, as she should. Drocco still couldn't keep his eyes off her and found himself thinking back to the smile she had given the clerk. He had initially thought that nothing about her pleasing features stood out as being remarkable, but he had been wrong—her smile was. It had enhanced her petite features so beautifully and even in the short glimpse he witnessed, it was mesmerizing. It infuriated him that he hadn't received anything close to a smile from her in all this time—over a month of watching her—yet he was the only one who deserved it. He was the fucking emperor. He brooded in his seat, considering if he should take her to bed that very night, but one thought of the Omegas threw that notion away. He had to figure out why the Omegas had been dying, and why his father and grandfather failed to mention it. Cailyn was the route to that knowledge.

He stared at her, a dark mood crawling over him at the restrictions on him. He would fuck her raw as soon as the investigation ended. The moment they found the Omegas, he would drag Cailyn into his— His thoughts shuddered to a stop. When they found the Omegas he would need to prioritize selecting the one that belonged him. He wouldn't have time for Cailyn. Fuck! He ground his teeth, his eyes boring into her. He wanted that smile on him, that body underneath him, that bouncy hair in his fist.

He descended into deep thought while the carriage swayed, jostling them about as it entered the cobbled palace grounds. Maybe he could keep her around and fuck her just before he bonded with his Omega. There wouldn't be much time though; he would need to complete the bond as soon as possible.

When the carriage arrived at the palace, his frustrations were even stronger than when they had started the journey, and he retreated to the training grounds to work off his agitation. Later that night, he tried again to find relief in the throat of a Beta female, but once again, he had to send her away without even undoing his pants. He could think of nothing but the smile that had not been for him.

"Greetings, King Malloron."

"Greetings, Emperor Drocco."

The portal hovered in front of Drocco, a transparent slash of vibrant energy through which he finally saw his only real adversary. King Malloron. The man certainly seemed to be a formidable looking Alpha. Wide and muscled, he was similar in stature to Drocco only with slightly browner skin and a more relaxed look in his dark eyes, but when dealing with a man who specialized in tricks, looks meant nothing. Drocco stood firm, broad arms crossed, staring at the richly dressed man through the portal. At least he wasn't wearing a ridiculous crown like the King of Ashens had.

"May Eiros thrive and be wealthy," Drocco said, reciting the mantra of Eiros.

"And may the mighty Lox Empire remain eternally dominant and just," King Malloron returned.

Around the edges of the room, behind the portal, three black-robed Talent-crafters gathered. They clasped hands with each other, linking them together as they watched the portal. Torin stood with them observing.

"I'm pleased we finally have a chance to talk," King Malloron added.

"As am I," Drocco replied, fully aware he did not sound pleased at all. "I want no misunderstandings developing about the Lox Empire and what its existence means for everyone else."

"I'm sure you don't," King Malloron said, inclining his head. "I just want to make it clear that I speak as ruler of Eiros, the largest and most developed territory in the Western Lands. I do not speak on behalf of any of the other territories here."

"Understood."

King Malloron dipped his head sharply. "Firstly, will you still allow trade across the White Ocean?"

"As long as traders are willing to be more open to declaring their wares, yes."

King Malloron lifted his head a touch. "Many of the old territories that are now under Lox ruling did not appreciate some of the more... unique wares the Western Lands had to offer. I wonder how lenient the Lox Empire will be?"

"You need not wonder, just ask," Drocco said, forcing himself to remain calm. Why didn't kings ever just speak plainly?

"Intoxicants like mutated wine, rare spirits, tobacco enhancers, recreational and medicinal substances including hallucinogens and Haze recreators," the king reeled off quickly.

"Fine as long as they are declared," Drocco said.

"Voluntary manual and sexual labor workers of any age?"

"Fine."

"Involuntary manual and sexual labor workers of any age?"

"Only criminals."

The king's eyebrows shot up and a slow smile spread across his face. "Agreed. What about goods that make use of the Talent?"

Drocco had to force himself not to flinch. "I'll need more time to consider that. Send a list of the kind of goods you're referring to and I'll think about it." He uncrossed his arms. "Regarding the proposal you made in your last letter, I fail to see how it would be a benefit to me."

The king sobered, his jaw becoming tight. "You don't see the value in acquiring the Talent?"

"What would I possibly need it for?" Drocco countered, dryly. "I don't spy—that activity has no honor. I'm also not interested in being an entertainer."

The king's nostrils flared and his whole body seemed to expand. "You think that is all the Talent is good for?"

Drocco remained silent, watching him with care. Much could be gleaned about a man when he burned in anger.

"I will assume you are unaware of whom you are speaking to, since my ancestors discovered and developed the Talent." The king's voice deepened and became harsher. "They were the first Talent-crafters to exist. The art has been honed and refined throughout the decades into something more powerful than anything any other Land could create. You may have experienced it through semi-skilled hacks and entertainers looking for quick coin, but I assure you, the Talent can do wondrous and incredible things, especially by an accomplished crafter." He leaned forward. "It could instantly unify your Empire without the need for Lox warriors in every city. It could aid you in finding the Omegas. It could seek out the perfect Omega for each Alpha. Imagine that," he said, his eyes narrowing with his intense expression. "Imagine if every Alpha could instantly locate their true mate?" He shook his head and leaned back. "You cannot say you truly understand the Talent if, as the ruler of such a powerful nation, you're telling me you don't want or need it."

Drocco held his eye and kept his stance unchanged while he thought carefully. Although he was fully aware of Malloron's obvious performance, he couldn't automatically refuse anything that might help him find the Omegas. "If the Talent can do all that, why haven't you done it?"

The king shook his head. "I willingly admit that the Talent cannot do everything," he said, his voice quieter. "The Talent is used in ways here that would interfere with any kind of use of that scale. Plus there are many accomplished crafters here." He smiled ruefully. "If my ancestors had been smarter, they wouldn't have given the knowledge away so freely. But the point is, the Western Lands are not united under one ruler like the Eastern Lands are now. In the Lox Empire, the Talent would catapult you to the greatest ruler history will ever know."

Drocco said nothing. Without a deeper understanding of the Talent, he had no idea if that was true or not but he wouldn't be coerced by empty statements aimed to stroke his ego.

"All I'm asking for in return is some of your warriors and training practices," the king continued, observing Drocco.

"My warriors are with me by choice, Malloron," Drocco said, dropping the formal title. He noticed Malloron stiffen very slightly—clearly he didn't like it. "I don't force them to stay and I will not force them to go."

"They stay with you because of your ridiculous vow to give each of them an Omega," Malloron snapped. "The only way you would even be able to do that is to make use of the Talent." He glared at Drocco. "All I want is your process of creating such a formidable army. It is an excellent trade considering the multiple uses of the Talent."

"Yes, unless you build an army to rival mine and decide to cross the White Ocean," Drocco shot back. "Then it would be a shit trade, wouldn't it? I would be handing you the potential knowledge to overthrow me."

Malloron's mouth tightened as he glared at Drocco, both of them remaining locked in a hot gaze.

"Eventually your army will leave you and you will be vulnerable, Drocco," Malloron glowered, rising from his seat. "All I need to do is wait until that day. You would be a fool to also wait until then. I'll give you a month to reconsider."

The portal shimmered brighter and then faded into nothing.

Drocco turned to Torin and watched the Talent-crafters release their hold on each other and begin to discuss. He had never truly considered using the Talent to aid him in ruling his Empire. In fact, the Lox had been ordered to cut down any and all Talent-crafters until Torin had pointed out that he would need them to defend against Malloron's sneaky intrusions. The most skilled Talent-crafters in the Eastern Lands had been offered the chance to pledge their loyalty to the Lox, which involved offering the life of a family member as a sacrificial gift, but Drocco had no idea how skilled they actually were. According to Malloron, skill was everything.

After speaking with the crafters, Torin approached him.

"Did you get what you needed?" Drocco asked.

"Yes," he said. "They say they have enough information now to find a way to block the Talent in a specific enclosed area."

"How long will it take?"

"A week or two. Where would you like them to set it up?"

"The Great Hall."

Torin raised an eyebrow. "For the celebration?"

"Exactly. We will have visitors from all territories. It's the perfect time to test loyalties. They only have five days to do it."

Torin nodded and was silent for a moment. "Do you want to discuss Malloron's offer?"

"I need to know more about how the Talent works before I can make any decision."

"From what I understand from our Lox crafters, the Talent is the ability to affect and manipulate the magic that surrounds and penetrates everything that exists," Torin explained. "The magic responds to 'spells,' which can be formed using certain words in the Ancient Tongue or certain actions of the hands, but is most powerful when bent by will. The mind has to reach a certain level of thought vibration to affect it by will."

"Thought vibration…" Drocco muttered. "This is why most Talent-crafters go insane at a young age."

Torin nodded. "The most skilled ones tend to, yes. And it's why most tend to use word or hand spells."

Drocco nodded, deep in thought.

"Would you like to meet with the Talent-crafters? They can explain it better than I can."

"Not right now," Drocco said, turning away from him. He hadn't been to see Cailyn that morning and a pressing urge to visit the research room had risen. "Make sure they are working on protecting the Great Hall by the time of the celebration."

CHAPTER FOUR

CAILYN

Cailyn was pleased that a plan had been arranged for her to leave Ashens.

Initially, she had been worried that the Records Keep staff would know that she wasn't Miss Lefroy, but she should have known that the Mothers had assistance in every area of the Eastern Lands. An Omega male she knew from a prior job worked at the Keep. Of course, he had blocks too and came across as a Beta in every way. He was one of the "dynamic variants" the head keeper had referred to and, for him, it was just as dangerous to reveal his true dynamic as it was for her.

Male Omegas were rare, and even more so since their families tended to murder them after discovering their dynamic. When the female Omegas began to disappear, the birth rate of male Omegas seemed to slow, and many had thought they were taken too, but in fact, they were simply being protected by the Mothers until they could protect themselves. Most of them led peaceful lives throughout the Lands, assisting the Mothers however they could.

Her Omega contact at the Keep had been awaiting her arrival with a plan in place to assist her cover. He was sure he could arrange an exit strategy for her and had been in the middle of explaining it when Drocco stormed over like the savage he was.

His need for control was stifling, as was his distrust of anyone who was not Lox. He watched her in the research room for hours every day, his imposing presence making her acutely aware of him. And then, when he wasn't there, the room had an imposing absence that she didn't like either. The day after the visit to the Records Keep he hadn't been in the room much and the wide, heavy chair in the corner he normally sat in remained empty. More than once, Cailyn caught herself standing in the room with files in her hands staring at it and... thinking about him.

Although her body hadn't physically reacted, it wasn't a good sign. Her blocks were still firmly in place and to be having an instinctual reaction to him when he wasn't even in the room was highly worrying. All she could do was hope that the Mothers had an answer. She couldn't continue to be an effective spy if her blocks were compromised.

In truth, he still terrified and disgusted her, but there was something else about him—something in his dark eyes, his confident manner, his steadfast conviction. She couldn't pinpoint it and wasn't sure if she even wanted to. Every moment she wasted thinking about him was a moment lost. All she had to do was remember what they discovered at the Records Keep to remind herself of that.

She had always known about the Omegas' suffering but never had she imagined that it had caused a death rate to such an extreme. It was horrific. That knowledge alone kept her pushing herself to focus. She had been covertly copying relevant files, even with the emperor in the room. Since he wanted her to make comments on his files, it became a good cover to make her own copies.

Two days after the visit, the communication she had been waiting for arrived. In her stack of fresh blank parchment, one sheet had a very slight sheen, glistening more than the others. Watching the closed door, she headed over to the desk in the far corner and sat on the floor, obscuring herself out of sight in case the emperor entered.

She placed the parchment flat on the floor and focused her mind. Searching the tightly woven layers of magic threaded into the sheet of parchment, she identified the extremely subtle indicators that showed the correct order to unravel it. As she did so, the message appeared:

Exit strategy not possible. You have his attention.
Routine will impede escape.
When distraction is achieved, create signal.

Cailyn closed her eyes immediately for a short moment and then opened them and read the message again. As her eyes reached the end, it faded and the ink began to flake away. She got up and brushed the parchment until it was clean. She stood for a moment, dismay thudding through her as she thought about the implication of the message. She wouldn't be getting out of there while everything in the palace ran routinely. Only a distraction would allow her to slip away unnoticed and signal for help. She sighed, throwing down the parchment. She had told her contact at the Keep that the emperor watched her constantly and he seemed to think it would still be fine. Why was having his attention suddenly a problem?

She thought for a long while, before realizing she was staring at his damn chair again. Cursing, she busied herself copying the last of the important files she needed while trying to think up a plan. A distraction was needed, but what? She would never be able to get out of the research room and create it without being noticed. The Lox Palace was huge, and even though she's studied its plans, she hadn't ever explored it. One wrong turn and she could end up anywhere.

Her mood sunk lower and by the afternoon she became angry with herself that she hadn't thought of anything. This kind of task was similar to the training exercises she used to thrive on. And now she couldn't think up one single escape distraction.

When Emperor Drocco entered, she actually scowled at him, agitated by the disturbance of her thinking time and annoyed that he had taken so long to come to her today.

He slowed to a stop at the sight of her expression, his eyes narrowing. "Is there something you wish to say?" It wasn't so much a question as a demand.

"No." She forced herself to answer in a mild manner when she really wanted to scream at him. "No, Emperor," she added, politely, before going back to her work.

He remained still and silent for a long while as she moved back and forth to the tables, then she heard him lowering into his chair.

A couple of days later, Cailyn stood in her living room by the glass wall, staring out over the city as the burnt orange sun lowered behind the smooth, jagged, uneven skyline. Ashens had been one of the prettier cities in the Eastern Lands before the war between King Thororm of Ashens and the Lox began. There seemed to be no reason for its destruction. Many theories circled around the emperor's dispute with the late king, but nothing had been confirmed by either party. Now it was a city of contrasts; the broken next to the beauty, the loyal among the traitors, the truth in plain sight among those that had been conditioned not to see.

Cailyn sighed and sipped her water while she returned her thoughts to the options for the distraction she needed. She hadn't come up with any strong ideas, only mediocre ones. She shouldn't really take a chance when dealing with Emperor Drocco, but she really wanted to get out of the palace. She had hardly seen Drocco lately and without his presence, she had sped up the copying of the files and sent everything to the Mothers with a note of her own. It was time to go.

A heavy knock fell on the door, startling her out of her thoughts. She made her way over to collect her dinner and found herself looking at an empty-handed young man.

"You have been summoned by Emperor Drocco, Miss Lefroy."

Cailyn's brows rose. "Why?"

The man widened his eyes at her question and instantly she realized he wouldn't know. Of course, no one questioned the emperor.

"Is he expecting me right now?"

"Yes, Miss Lefroy."

Cailyn sighed. Taking a moment to ensure she was presentable, she followed the servant through a number of corridors and stopped outside an intricately engraved set of double doors.

"You may enter, Miss Lefroy," the man said, gesturing to the door.

Cailyn took a moment to compose herself before entering.

She stepped into a large room with heavy multi-colored rugs, cream walls and windows along the back wall letting in the last of the evening sun. A mahogany dining table sat on one side of the room and the emperor sat at the head, watching her as she entered.

"How may I help you, Emperor," Cailyn asked, lowering her head.

"You are to dine with me," he said, his cold gaze taking her in. "Take a seat."

Cailyn glanced up, confused. He planned to have dinner with her? "Excuse me for being bold,

Emperor," she began, "but I have a lot of work to do—"

"You are done for the day," the emperor stated, as though bored. He poured red liquid from a glass jug into two glasses.

"Emperor," Cailyn said, trying again. "I really need to be spending all my time working if I'm to meet the dead—"

"So you were working in your quarters?" He served her a glare, placing the jug down. "With files I told you not to remove from the research room?"

"No, Emperor."

"Then you are available," he said. "And from what I understand, you were awaiting your dinner."

Cailyn mumbled confirmation that she had been and then pressed her lips together to avoid saying anything more. She moved to the other end of the table, only to discover that the only other chair at the table, apart from the emperor's, was positioned on the corner right next to him. She hesitated. Normally a visitor of equal standing would sit opposite the host, while a visitor of lesser standing or an employee might sit a few seats down along one side. They were certainly not seated next to the host like their confidant, lover, or mate. He was making a statement by removing all the chairs.

"You will sit here," Emperor Drocco said, gesturing to the other chair after she hesitated too long.

She glanced around the room for any other chairs, but the rest of the furniture consisted of plush, teal couches, end tables, and short bookcases.

"Sit," ordered the Alpha.

"Are there no other chairs?" she asked. She couldn't be so close to him again.

"They are not needed," he said, his voice deepening. "You will sit here."

Annoyed with his demand, and frustrated with her lack of choice, a retort slipped out of her before she had time to even think about it. "If you're having a problem securing furniture, I could arrange help for you, Emperor. There's no need to live like a foolish market trader."

The man's entire body tensed and his eyes slipped into a darkness she hadn't seen before. Instantly, she reined in her scowl and hurried toward the chair. As she sat down he grabbed her jaw and yanked her face close to his.

"That is the last fucking time you will speak to me in that way, kitten," he rumbled. "I have been extremely lenient with your attitude, as I'm sure you recognize, but it is becoming tiresome. Am I clear?"

She stared at his face looming in front of her and nodded, unable to speak with her jaw tight in his grip.

"Good." He slowly let go of her but kept his face close. As his eyes flitted over her face, the look in them changed, and there it was—that feeling again.

Cailyn leaned back, away from him, and took a breath, resisting the urge to rub her jaw. She turned her attention to the table. A number of jugs filled with water and other colored liquids had been placed among empty plates and bowls.

The emperor clapped his hands and a line of servants entered bringing with them steaming bowls and plates of food.

Cailyn's mouth watered as the delicious spicy aromas filled the room. She stared at the numerous plates and bowls being placed down on the table; cold and hot slices of spiced meat, curried and baked potatoes, fragrant stews of all colors, buttered greens, crusty charcoaled bread, mashed roots, and even delicacies like peppered cow tongue, jellied purple eggs, and cracked claw.

"Do you eat like this all the time?" she asked the emperor, in wonder.

"Not really," he said. "I wasn't sure what you ate. Pick what you'd like."

Cailyn selected a small range of dishes to try and began to eat cautiously.

"What progress have you made so far?" The emperor asked, spooning meat stew into his mouth.

Cailyn kept her eyes down. "I found reference to information about the Alpha/Omega connection."

"Yes." The emperor hesitated. "Is that of importance?"

"I'm not sure," Cailyn said. "It could be. No current living Alpha has ever been with an Omega, have they?"

Emperor Drocco let out a growl that caused her to glance up at him. "No. What has this got to do with the investigation?"

"I was thinking that maybe an Alpha that had bonded with an Omega could be used to locate her."

"No, that theory has already been disproved," he said. "Wherever the Omegas go, it isn't possible for their mates to locate them."

"Hmm…" Cailyn said, feigning thoughtfulness.

"What?"

"Well, that in itself is interesting. There are very few places where the connection cannot be felt."

"I never said the connection could not be felt," the emperor said. "The connection can indeed be felt, very deeply. I'm willing to guess that the bonded Omegas who were taken suffered greatly."

Cailyn watched him. He seemed to be agitated even discussing it, but this was one of the things she needed to know. She had to press him. "How do you know?"

The emperor chewed slowly for a long while, and Cailyn thought for a moment he wasn't going to answer. "I knew an Alpha who had bonded with an Omega who was taken," he said, finally. "He felt their connection every day, right up to the day of his death. The loss of her changed him, distorted him, made him vastly different to who he had been. I can only imagine the same fate fell on her." His face clouded over as he spoke and Cailyn couldn't look away from his eyes. They were stormy and hard yet tinged with something so slight she almost missed it; a subdued mellowness. It made his entire expression different. She couldn't think clearly to ask her next question, so she kept quiet until she had eaten her fill.

"You don't eat enough, kitten," he commented, pushing his plate away.

The servants returned to collect the dishes and their plates.

"It's Cailyn, Emperor."

He turned to look at her, his gaze intense. "I know."

She made a face. "You keep calling me kitten."

"Yes, that's what you are."

Cailyn struggled not to bristle. He had given her a nickname as though she was his whore. Coupled with where she had been placed at the table, the insult was too great for her to remain quiet. "At the risk of insulting you, Emperor, I'd like to point out we are not familiar with each other in that way."

The emperor leaned forward. "Incorrect. I'm completely familiar with the kind of Beta you are."

"And what kind am I?" she asked, evenly.

"The kind who likes to show their claws and nip and scratch, and make noise for the sake of it," he said. "But ultimately, doesn't make any real impact."

Cailyn's anger rose steadily. "So you're saying I'm useless?"

The bastard had the nerve to smirk at her, his black eyes gleaming. "Even kittens have their uses."

"Because they're entertaining?" she spat. "Nice to look at and easily pacified?"

The emperor broke into a grin as she spoke.

"Because they can be put in their place and are easy to confuse and distract?" She glared at him, grinding her teeth in annoyance.

He threw his head back, releasing peals of husky laughter.

Cailyn sat and fumed. He had already warned her of her impertinence and saying anything else would certainly cause her to be punished, but she found that she didn't care. "I wonder if that's how you see the Omegas you seek. Playthings to brush aside when you get tired of them."

"An Omega has a lifetime duty to her Alpha just as an Alpha has a lifetime duty to his Omega," he said, still chuckling. "It is a unique connection. You would do well to stop trying to understand it."

At least he perceived Omegas as special, even if they were to be akin to breeding machines for his men. "Yes," she muttered. "I think I will. Thank the stars I'll be bonding with a Beta and not have to deal with being seen as ineffective and dumb."

The heavy chuckle from the emperor stopped abruptly. "Are you betrothed?"

"Why? Do you not think a Beta would be interested in a dumb little kitten?" she said, unable to help the retort.

"I asked you a question," he snapped, his eyes suddenly hard.

She glared at him but backed down when she noticed the wildness in his eyes. He was angry. "No," she said, tightly.

He relaxed back into his chair, observing her.

A servant entered and hovered by the door. "Would you like dessert, your Imperial Majesty?"

Cailyn stood up before he could answer. "I'm heading back to my quarters, Emperor. Thank you for dinner. Is there anything else?"

The emperor's jaw constricted and he straightened in his chair. "Sit down."

Cailyn sat and waited while the emperor told the servants to bring dessert.

"There will be a celebration in a few days marking the Lox victory in the Eastern Lands," he said.

Cailyn's interest peaked but she avoided reacting.

"Rulers of all the territories in the Eastern Lands will be attending, as will many Lox warriors. All who are in the palace will be loyal to the Lox."

There it was—her distraction. "It sounds like it will be an enjoyable event, Emperor," she said, demurely. "I will not be a disturbance to you or any of your people during that time."

"You will attend," the emperor said. "And you will pledge your allegiance to the Lox."

Cailyn jolted in her seat, her eyes snapping up to his. "What?"

The emperor's eyes bore into her. "All who remain in the palace must be loyal to the Lox."

"I'm happy to give you my word about my loyalty, Emperor," Cailyn said, as her horror rose. "But I cannot pledge it. I only have my sister. I will not sacrifice her just to make you feel more comfortable to have me here. I'll leave if that's what you need."

Occasionally an innocent person would be caught up in the missions she undertook, but Miss Lefroy's sister was only eight. Cailyn had always ensured that children were never affected by her missions, and this would not be the exception.

"And where will you go? The entire Eastern Lands is now Lox Empire. You won't be able to escape pledging your allegiance and I will not end your employment."

The servants reentered with more plates and bowls, but Cailyn's eyes remained on Drocco. This expectation on her to pledge to the Lox would ruin her cover.

"Most of the files are organized now. A team of historians could find patterns one mind would miss," she suggested.

Drocco didn't even answer her. He bit into a slice of black crumble cake and chewed, watching her.

"I'm sure the keepers would also be very useful in assisting—"

"I'm not ending your employment."

"You cannot kill my sister," she countered.

"I will have your loyalty."

"You have it," she hissed, leaning forward. "Just don't hurt my sister."

"It is the way of the Lox," Drocco said, somewhat nonchalantly. "It is the only way to ensure true loyalty."

"Do you intend to ask everyone to pledge?" she asked, her voice rising. "Your entire Empire? Because you'll have no one left."

"Just the people who have access to this building," he said, taking another bite and shooting her a look that said he had noticed her tone.

Cailyn fought against the effect his glance had on her, choosing to focus on the utter disgust at his methods. This man had no business running an Empire. It would indeed be dark times ahead for the people of the Eastern Lands.

"Your sister will be brought here for the ceremony," Drocco said, once he'd finished the cake.

"No!" Cailyn tried a different tack and burst into tears. "No, Emperor, please."

"The quicker you accept it, the quicker you can move on," he said, irritably.

Cailyn's anger built steadily. Of course he wouldn't be affected by tears, the man had no compassion. She quietened and began picking at a bowl of fruit. They ate in silence for a while until Drocco had finished, and Cailyn stopped the pretense of eating.

"A dress has been left in your quarters that I expect you to wear to the celebration," Drocco said, as the last plates were cleared. "I have been told it's in your size."

Cailyn took a sip of the spiced tea that had been poured for her. "Yes, Emperor."

As soon as he dismissed her, Cailyn returned to her quarters and pulled a sheet of parchment from her writing equipment. Clearing her mind, she gently filtered magic into the ink of her quill-pen as she wrote.

Prepare for distraction. Signal will follow.
Protect loved one or unwanted reveal inevitable.

She inspected the ink and, once satisfied, sealed the parchment with magic. This hid the ink, protected the message from the casual Talent-crafter, and made it a beacon for her contact. She folded it and placed it in the trash. If Miss Lefroy's sister suddenly went on a trip or in some way became inaccessible, there would be no one else for the emperor to threaten her with.

She entered her bedroom and noticed the dress laid out on the bed. It was a close fitted, long dress with a slashed neckline that would reveal the tops of her shoulders. Cailyn fingered the soft deep red material. It was beautiful, of course, and reminded her of the sophisticated stateswomen and regal royals she had seen during her work in various cities. She never thought she would ever dress in such quality material or in such a graceful design.

She pulled her hand back sharply. She would be leaving the night of the celebration. As soon as she showed her face for the emperor to tell her that her pledge would be delayed, she would escape. He would be too busy drinking himself into a stupor and fucking his Lox women to notice anything.

She dropped onto the bed breathing a sigh of relief. She was going home.

CHAPTER FIVE

DROCCO

The Great Hall had been decorated to Drocco's liking. The elaborate ornamentation and gleaming weaponry on display reflected the impressive Lox might and wealth. Thick, long tables had been organized in the space, as well as circular areas with plush seating to watch dancers, musicians, and single combat challenges. Lox colors—red and black—coordinated the entire display and were echoed in the chosen clothing of his most experienced warriors who prowled the hall like wild animals.

Drocco noticed his visitors were very nervous anytime a warrior sat near them or even passed by. It was a good sign. Fear was one of his greatest weapons.

The evening was going well. He hadn't yet spoken to all the rulers of his territories but they were all in attendance. Some had bought their nominated family member in preparation for their pledge and others didn't yet realize that a random family member had already been collected for that required purpose. Annoyingly, there had been three whose family members had proved difficult to reach, including the historian's sister. He had demanded to know if she had sent any communication out of the palace since their dinner, but it had been reported back that she hadn't. It didn't matter though. He would get her sister eventually.

Family sacrifices were the most effective way to weaken a family structure and ensure the whole family felt threatened enough to pledge loyalty to him. Cailyn might not have any other family, but he wanted her unwavering loyalty. And she would give it to him. Maybe not tonight, but it would happen.

Drocco sat up on the platform watching the festivities in the Great Hall become rowdier as the evening wore on. The wide, heavy throne he rested in had been a gift from the Grence cities who were known and celebrated for their quality furniture and upholstery. It was positioned in the center of the platform with only a small table to his left where his tankard of ale sat. Before the platform stood a row of guards. Every so often, a warrior would pass and call to him to join in; to eat, applaud the dancers, encourage those in combat, and boast their achievement. Drocco would cheer and call back to them, but the guards would wave them on so he wasn't too disturbed.

His Talent-crafters claimed that each entrance to the Great Hall had been fitted with a charm, made of a collection of specific gems and crystals, that would disable any use of the Talent within the hall. Of course, that wouldn't tell him if any of his visitors used it, but it should prevent anything untoward from happening at the event. He watched Torin move through the crowd, his steel eyes taking everything in. There was a chair for him on a separate lower stage on the far left, but Torin never sat idle. At least Drocco could count on Torin to see the things he wouldn't.

As the time for pledges drew closer, Drocco became restless. The celebration wasn't lifting his spirits as he thought it would. All it did was remind him that there was a long way to go to unite the Empire. The challenges still remained; eliminating the small resistance who remained loyal to the dead King of Ashens, solving the puzzle of the missing Omegas, and uniting all the territories under his rule. He looked forward to tackling them but the celebration felt like it was at the wrong time. He should be spending time working on his investigation. He glanced around. Cailyn hadn't yet arrived. He sent for her and then stood to give his celebration speech for his warriors and visitors. He spoke with all the passion and fire and impatience bounding through him, and the hall erupted with crazed roars and boisterous cheers.

As he sat down, he saw Cailyn enter. He couldn't take his eyes from her as she threaded through the crowd toward him. He almost held his breath as he stared. The woman was utterly gorgeous. Her hair had been swept up again revealing that delicate neck, and the dress clung to every delicious curve. Finally he could see her luscious figure in detail and it had been worth the wait. With the cut of the dress revealing the tops of her shoulders, her simple elegance seemed out of place among the raucous crowd.

His guards let her through at his instruction and she climbed the platform and stood before him, her head low.

"I'm not pleased you had to be summoned, kitten," he said, lifting his ale and keeping his eyes on her.

"I'm sure you can understand I wasn't eager to attend, considering your plans to..." Her voice petered out, her head lifted and she closed her eyes, swaying slightly. Then her eyes opened, widening as an expression of horror seeped into her face.

Drocco frowned, confused, and then a scent hit him. A rich, luscious, sublime scent, like nothing he had smelled before. It penetrated every part of him, causing a yearning so powerful that suddenly every fiber of his being switched to high alert.

"No," Cailyn whispered, taking a step back. "No. It can't..."

Drocco ignored her and leaned forward, trying to decipher what he was experiencing. A fog began to swamp his mind, and the only clear thought emerging was that he needed that scent—it belonged to him. He turned his head slowly seeking it out, and then snapped back to Cailyn. It was her.

Cailyn glanced around wildly as she backed away, her whole body tense and poised to bolt.

Drocco rose slowly, every inch of him aware of every inch of her. A raw hunger developed as he took in her terrified expression, her scent blossoming into an aroma so enticing, so complex, his cock hardened to rock. At the same time, the guards behind her began to turn and look at her, their nostrils flaring.

Something snapped in Drocco. He swept forward and lifted Cailyn, throwing her over his shoulder before storming out of the Great Hall. He maneuvered through the corridors of the palace to the nearest private space he could find, trying to ignore the sweet aroma filling his nostrils. He could barely think. All he knew was that he needed to be alone with her. His guards would be following him; he wanted to lose them.

He arrived at his barely used office and entered without breaking his stride. Heading to the center of the room, he put her down, keeping his hands on her soft body as he breathed her in.

She looked up at him and he froze. Her brown irises had morphed to include a hint of gold—a gold he had only ever read about, a gold that no one had seen in one hundred and eleven years.

"Are you an Omega?" he said, his voice hoarse with disbelief.

She took advantage of his shock to stumble away from him to the far wall. "What did you do?" she cried. She pressed herself up against the wall and almost sobbed. "They're gone. They're all gone! What did you do?"

Drocco watched her eyes turning more golden as the seconds passed. "Explain yourself, Cailyn Lefroy," he demanded. "Are you an Omega, or have you taken something?"

The woman moved along the wall and then back again, looking around frantically. Her scent seeped into the room almost lazily, and it called to Drocco to cease all the questioning and rip that dress off of her. But he forced himself to resist. He needed to

75

know what had changed. How could she suddenly smell so good and have acquired the infamous golden eyes of an Omega in her Haze? Was it a trick? Hadn't Malloron mentioned Haze recreators coming into the city more often? She could be trying to trap him as revenge for her sister. And yet, as Drocco continued to watch her, she became more desperate.

"Tell me," he demanded. "Are you an Omega?"

She bent over, pressing her hands between her legs, and groaned. That groan shuddered through him, and his already hard cock jumped painfully. He stepped toward her.

Her head snapped up. "Don't move!" she snarled at him, holding out a hand. "Don't come near me."

Drocco stopped, tilting his head to observe her. Although his mind was clouded, he forced himself to think.

If she were trying to trap him she wouldn't want him to stay away from her. Plus, he had never known of any Haze imitation drug that caused such a powerful scent; in fact, nothing that existed caused the golden eyes... which meant she was truly an Omega. Amazement leapt through him, quickly followed by a blast of glee. He smiled.

The door opened behind him.

"Is everything okay, your Imperi—"

"Guard the door," he bellowed at the guard, his eyes still on Cailyn. "No one is to enter. No one."

The guard sniffed once. "Yes, your Imperial Majesty."

The door closed again and Drocco stood in a wide stance, his arms crossed, watching every move Cailyn made. If this woman was truly an Omega, she was going into her Haze. It was unstoppable and would render her incapable of anything but the need to mate. He had already been waiting for her for so long, it was almost poetic that he would finally get to experience her in this most beautiful state. And not only that, she would come to him—no submission training necessary. For all her defiance and strength of personality, she would have no control over wanting him. His questions could wait. He intended to enjoy every moment of what was to come.

CHAPTER SIX

CAILYN

Cailyn fought against the oncoming Haze with all her might, but she knew it was in vain. In all her years at the compound, she had never felt the onset of the Haze as strongly as she did now. It didn't help that the deep, musky scent of Alpha surrounded her.

Since she had entered the Great Hall, something within her hadn't felt right but she ignored it, eager to get her meeting with the emperor over with. As she stood in front of him, his heady scent had hit her. No longer bland, it shuddered through her and almost knocked out every other sense. Her body reacted immediately. It shouldn't have happened. When she searched for her blocks, they had simply disappeared—every single one of them.

She glanced around the room again for any possible way of escaping, but the only available exit was the one Drocco had just told his guards to block. Her panic and fear rocketed. If she went into the Haze right now she would most certainly be a slave for the rest of her life. She thought hard, even as the trembling took over her whole body. Slick gathered between her legs and her golden sight had almost fully bloomed.

She moved against the wall, sure that Drocco was going to simply take her in hand and fuck her as viciously as she imagined, but he didn't even move. He simply watched her.

She gritted her teeth and tensed as her trembling increased. The fucking bastard was waiting—waiting for her to go fully into her Haze when she wouldn't resist him. She needed a way out.

"You will tell me everything I need to know," Drocco said, the triumph in his voice as clear as his desire. "You can try to fight it as long as you need to, but it will happen."

Cailyn pressed her hands against the wall as she glared at him, forcing down the retort on her tongue. In her current state, she could say anything, and every single Omega in existence needed her to keep her mouth shut. As she glared at him, a plan formed. She looked around the room again, noting its shape and furniture. She only had one shot, and time was running out.

She pushed off the wall and walked toward him. He suddenly stilled, his arms uncrossing as she tentatively approached. His black eyes were wilder than she had ever seen them and his nostrils flared with every step she took.

"Yes," Drocco murmured. "Come to me, kitten. Accept your situation."

Cailyn breathed shallowly as she reached him, trying not to take in too much of his scent. Lifting her hands, she dug her nails into his neck and clawed down. She scratched him down to his shoulders, digging in hard until small trails of blood burst forth in their wake. "Do not call me kitten!"

Drocco didn't even flinch. In fact, he smiled. "Your claws are ineffective, kitten, just as I've always told you. You're even more a kitten now than you were before."

He grabbed her wrists and lowered his head to sniff her and breathe along her arm.

She watched, becoming transfixed with the look of pleasure on his face at this simple action.

"You are almost in your Haze," he murmured. He glanced at her, a smirk on his lips. "In a moment you will agree with everything I say, you will do everything I say, and you will think I'm the best thing that exists."

Cailyn snatched her arms out of his hands and backed away. He watched her, his smirk deepening as she took a breath and focused her mind.

One thing about using the Talent was that it forced crafters to train their mental ability to ignore sensory distractions. Once in her Haze, she would barely be able to even think clearly, let alone use the Talent, so anything she was going to do had to be done now. Calling forth the magic in the room, including the energy within Drocco's exposed blood, she backed into a corner of the office and weaved together a sophisticated magical shield that stretched from one wall to the other, locking her into the corner. It solidified, and she let out a breath as she released her mental hold. She stepped forward and placed a hand on it. It was strong and sturdy and would most likely last for as long as her Haze did.

She slumped to the floor in relief. At the sound of stomping footsteps, she looked up to see Drocco slam a hand on the glistening barrier between them. His face distorted. "What have you done?" he bellowed. "You have the Talent? Undo this now!"

She stared at him, pressing her mouth together so she wouldn't speak. Without her blocks, she was susceptible to his demands, but she would work hard to not say anything.

He flew into a rage, punching the barrier over and over as he roared in fury.

Cailyn shifted back until she was as far away from him as possible. She should have included a sound barrier so that she wouldn't be able to hear him, but at least she couldn't smell any more of him than was already in her small area. His every yell of anger bolted through her, putting her on edge, but there was only so much she could do in this state. The ideal scenario would be if she could still signal her contact or somehow get out of the palace. She sat up straight, suddenly realizing something. She stood, ignoring the idiot Alpha still pounding the barrier. Trying to focus her mind, she began to create the portal against the wall. She had to go slower so that she could get the casting correct. Since she did not use speech or even actions, her mind needed to be sturdy for the spell to work and her Haze was so close that she wasn't sure if it would. A rectangle of light shone on the wall for a moment and then faded away.

Drocco's yelling behind her changed, became more urgent, but she ignored him. His own blood made up the barrier; he wouldn't be able to get through and it was unlikely any other weaker Alpha would either. She had basically protected herself from everyone in the building. She doubted the Lox Talent-crafters would be able to get through. She knew for certain that every Omega in her compound was more skilled than Talent-crafters in the Eastern Lands.

She tried the portal again, but this time it didn't even gleam. Her mind was becoming a complete muddle and she could barely think past the scent of Alpha that still filled her every inhale. She dropped onto the floor, moaning as the familiar thrum of need trembled through her whole body. This was it.

It was warm. She lifted her dress up to her waist and pulled her arms out of the wide-neck top. She panted and squeezed her legs together as her pussy throbbed. The smell of Alpha was everywhere, and yet no Alpha lay with her. It wasn't right.

She settled with her feet tucked under her, watching the Alpha across the room as he paced and watched her back, rumbling growls coming from him and a vicious snarl on his face. His black eyes were beautiful. They were like ink affected by magic— shiny, deep and bottomless—and they looked at her with a fierce desire that sent goosebumps over her whole body. Other Alphas were in the room, but she only watched him. Although the other men were also unbonded Alphas, her golden sight showed her the one with the most potential for breeding. And it was the one with the beautiful black eyes that had the richest, strongest glow. He was perfect to breed an unbonded Omega. To breed her. The men continued to talk, but she purposefully ignored their words, only focusing on the Alpha with the black eyes. His voice drew forth her slick, preparing her for him. She hoped that if she waited patiently, he would come for her.

However, as the hours went by, the other men left and he did nothing but pace and watch her. She made a noise of disgust and leaned forward onto her hands and knees. Her body ached with unspent release and she stretched, curving her back and lengthening her legs. Her slick ran down her thighs, and she couldn't hold off for the Alpha anymore. She lay on her back and widened her legs, slipping her fingers between them. A thunderous roar erupted in her ears and froze her still.

"Don't you fucking dare!" He was there, his face pushed up against the barrier as he stared down at her, his black eyes intense with fury.

She moved her fingers away, whimpering. His primitive behavior increased her desire for him and more slick flowed from her. His eyes flicked down her body and back up to her face. He said something else but she couldn't focus on anything but his glow. She needed an Alpha like him. He was the only one that would be able to quench the need building in her and nearly wrenching her apart, but he was choosing to leave her to suffer. What had she done wrong?

After a while, he stopped speaking. He watched her, pressed up against the barrier, and she watched him. She wasn't sure how many more moments, half hours, or hours went by but soon the need was too strong. She inched her fingers down between her legs and began to pleasure herself, ignoring the howling Alpha who would not do what he was supposed to.

CHAPTER SEVEN

DROCCO

Drocco paced his office as he watched the Omega, simmering with a violent blend of rage, desire, and desperation.

Of course, the historian had to be a fucking Talent-crafter as well as an Omega. She had been right under his nose and he had been too distracted by her beauty and willfulness to suspect a fucking thing. He didn't even put together that her scent had changed as soon as she entered the Great Hall. Clearly, the charms his Talent-crafters installed had worked. If his mind hadn't been so blurry, he would have noticed, and restrained her as soon as he had the chance. Instead, she was secured behind a barrier made of his own blood, torturing him.

He watched her come to yet another orgasm, her hips jerking into her hand as she lay on her side, her sighs and moans and undecipherable utterings sparking savage instincts and urges he had never experienced before. His rock-hard cock strained against his trousers, painful and needing release. The sight, smell, and sound of her made every part of him come alive, particularly that part of him.

He had tried everything to get the barrier down, but it remained solid. At his initial yells and roars, his warrior guards had entered, fearing for his safety. They tried to assist him, but ultimately any man who entered the room became incapable of thinking intelligently. The Omega's scent was so powerful that they became too distracted by her to do anything. He had already sunk his dagger into three of his men's throats and ripped it through their trachea for watching her too long. After that, only Torin was allowed in the room, and he had the sense to keep his back turned to Cailyn at all times.

"You haven't eaten in three days, Drocco," Torin said.

Drocco kept his eyes on Cailyn. "Neither has she."

"You already know that the Haze blocks out her appetite for food—many of her bodily functions have ceased."

Drocco turned to him, his simmering emotions bubbling up. "I will eat when she eats. Have you come with any solutions or are you just here to nag?"

"She isn't the real Miss Lefroy."

Drocco turned back to the writhing Omega on the floor. "Who is she?"

"I don't know yet. She seems to have come out of nowhere."

Drocco clenched his fists so hard, a shooting pain ricocheted up his arms. She had fooled him all this time. "Is she a spy from the Western Lands? Is she under orders from Malloron?"

"I don't think so. She hasn't been taking information or reporting to anyone while she's been in the palace," Torin said. "The Talent-crafters have confirmed that she hasn't been creating portals or using her Talent on any of the documents in the research room."

"That doesn't mean she isn't working for him," Drocco snapped.

"It is unlikely," Torin said. "She has been watched since she arrived. She doesn't behave like normal Western Lands spies behave."

Drocco exhaled harshly. That didn't mean anything. The fact that she used the Talent at all suggested she was sympathetic to Malloron's rule and influence, most Talent-crafters were.

"I would like to suggest that you don't make any assumptions about her before you are able to question her," Torin said, evenly.

Drocco turned to him again, his eyes narrowed. "You presume to tell me how to deal with this situation?"

"You are in your rut, Drocco," Torin said slowly and clearly. "A true rut for a real Omega. You are handling it well, but you're not thinking properly and we have already lost three men to that fact. There is much to learn from her."

Drocco closed his eyes and took a breath to calm his annoyance. Of course, that was true but why was Torin explaining the obvious? He opened his eyes. "This is the first real Omega that we have seen in the decades, Torin. Rut or no, I will be learning all that she knows."

"You are aware that she may know where the other Omegas are?"

"Do you think I'm a fool?" Drocco bellowed.

Cailyn whimpered and turned to look at him from the floor, her dress twisted around her marvelous body exposing a smooth breast. He stared at her, quickly losing interest in whatever he had been about to say to Torin.

"I'm just saying that this could be the exact push toward solving the mystery that the Lox need. Discipline is needed and I'm not sure that you will be able to withstand your own impulses. Our grandfathers told us about the preparation they went through before meeting their first Omegas. You have had none of that," Torin said. "I'm simply pointing out the importance of this. If you overpower her in your eagerness to—"

"I have not forgotten my duty to my army, Torin." Drocco interrupted, dragging his eyes from Cailyn. "But this Omega came directly to me. She is mine. Any impulses I have will be her burden to bear and she will take them like she is supposed to."

Torin held his eye. "Have you considered that maybe, if the barrier lasts longer than her Haze, she might create a working portal and escape before you get access to her?"

Drocco roared, a raging burn tearing through him at the very idea. He advanced on Torin, wild and ready to strike. "You had better make sure that doesn't *fucking* happen!"

"Then let me bring in the crafters," Torin said, unmoved by Drocco's state. "Let them come in to help us get the barrier down. Let them help you to keep her. They are the only ones that can make sure she doesn't get away."

Drocco paused in his tracks, battling the fuzziness in his mind to think through the logic of the suggestion. In his fit of rage at the barrier between him and his Omega, he had ordered all Lox crafters to be quartered, hung, burned, have their cocks ripped off by horses, and then be fed alive to wolves. Of course, it was a ridiculous order and Torin had ignored it. Despite Drocco's annoyance, some small sanity in him reminded him that they were the reason he had discovered her in the first place. They were loyal to him and would understand what she had done. She had already tried to create a portal before her Haze fully took over. He couldn't let her escape.

"I'll allow it," Drocco said, through gritted teeth.

Torin dipped his head in a nod and bowed before swiftly leaving the room, careful to keep his back to the Omega.

The Omega watched him leave, and Drocco growled at her, a surge of something unpleasant and raw rushing through him. She shouldn't be watching Torin. She hadn't watched any of the other Alphas that had entered the room. Her stunning deep-gold eyes snapped back to him and she fixed herself on her knees, sitting on her heels, and lowered her head.

"Kitten," Drocco began. "Undo the barrier."

She didn't look up.

"Kitten. Come to me."

Those eyes glanced up at him, caught his face and then her head rose slowly, her expression one of wonder. It mellowed him somewhat. It was though she found him fascinating and he was satisfied with that.

"Come to me."

She tilted her head, her eyes running over his face and then all the way down his body. She made a noise in the back of her throat and his cock jumped and leaked. He knew she wasn't hearing him because she had zero interest in anything he said, and he was unable to force her to listen. He had already tried ordering her, yelling at her, teasing her, enticing her—nothing worked. She was following pure instincts, instincts to entice an Alpha to fuck her. According to the reports, that was all an Omega in her Haze was able to think about. But he still spoke to her anyway.

"Kitten." Her eyes jumped back up to his face and her brow furrowed.

He could see now that she was an Omega. When he thought about everything he had read, she had all the features. She was small, she was beautiful, she had incredibly gorgeous hair, and her shapely, soft body was perfectly suited to breeding. The only thing that did not suit the Omega stereotype was her continuous disrespectful attitude—that was something that he had never heard of before in an Omega. But in her Haze none of that willfulness seemed to be present.

Drocco exhaled heavily and began to take off his clothes, unable to bear the strain any longer. Her scent still lingered in the room, and although he could not smell the shiny slick pooled on the floor behind the barrier, it was still enticing nonetheless. The Omega snapped to attention as soon as he began to reveal his body. When he pulled his pants down, she actually breathed a sigh as his cock sprung forth, the tip wet and dripping.

He stroked himself slowly. "Come to me, kitten." He breathed her scent in deep. "Come to me and get what you need."

The Omega leaned forward and began to crawl to him, her hips swaying behind her as she moved forward, her eyes on his cock. He moaned at the sight and more fluid dripped from his tip. She was so alluring, it was actual torture. Why the fuck had he waited?

When she reached the barrier, she pressed her palms on it rising up to her knees. She looked up at him, her golden gaze filled with desire and hope, her mouth slightly ajar.

"Come to me," he said, hoarsely, stroking himself faster. "Undo the barrier."

She frowned at him and looked back down at his cock as she pressed her forehead against the barrier.

"Undo it!"

Drocco's demand fell on deaf ears. Staring at his cock, the Omega opened her pretty, pink mouth and licked the barrier.

Fuck, he couldn't take it. Emitting a growl of frustration, Drocco found himself standing before her, bracing himself with a hand on the barrier as he stroked faster. Ripples of pleasure threaded through him and he kept his eyes on her as she continued licking in vain, trying to reach him. His crescendo rose quickly, jagged and intense. He exploded, his release shooting toward her mouth but hitting the barrier. His body jerked repeatedly, over and over, until he finally stilled, his fluids streaming down the barrier to the floor.

Drocco breathed heavily, his ears ringing. That had been more powerful than normal, and an enormous amount of semen ran down the barrier.

Cailyn stared at his release as it drained down, then looked up at him. The disappointment in her eyes tore through him.

"Take down the barrier, kitten," Drocco demanded, feeling himself already hardening again. "Take it down and you can have it."

She sat back on her heels for a moment, looking sorrowfully at his hardening cock, before turning and crawling back to the wall.

The next day, the Talent-crafters examined the barrier. Drocco watched them carefully, his dagger in hand. Not one of them looked at the Omega writhing on the floor beyond it, but Drocco remained on edge. As soon as they had finished examining, they left the room immediately and discussed with Torin outside. Cailyn brought herself to yet another orgasm and Drocco could do nothing but stare in frustration. In fact, he ached to pull his pants down and stroke himself to another powerful release, but that wouldn't help him right now. He needed to know what the Talent-crafters thought about the barrier, and a jittery nervousness entered him for the first time ever. He didn't like the feeling.

"Tell me," he demanded, the moment Torin re-entered the room. They had agreed to not tell the crafters that Cailyn was a Talent-crafter herself.

"They said that the barrier is strong and has indeed been infused with your blood as you suspected," Torin said, situating himself with his back to the Omega. "It has been created by an extremely skilled Talent-crafter, but they don't think that the crafter is from the Western Lands, something about the way the magic has been woven is unique; not something typical of the Western Lands or the Eastern Lands."

"What about the barrier?" Drocco snapped. He didn't give a shit about any of that other stuff right now. "How long is it going to last?"

Torin pressed his lips together disapprovingly, but said, "It is solid, Drocco. It will not allow any flesh to pass through it in either direction but it may allow for objects or food. They think it will last at least another eight days."

Drocco thought back to all of the reports he'd read about Omegas. How long did the Haze typically last for? As he tried to remember, he was distracted by Cailyn. She was back on her knees up against the barrier, looking at him with a pleading gaze. A hint of a smile appeared on her face. Drocco took a breath and held it, waiting to see if she would truly give him a smile.

"Drocco," Torin said. "Focus."

Drocco turned to him and blinked. What the hell had they been talking about?

"Eight more days for the barrier at least," Torin reminded him.

Drocco exhaled in frustration. "I can't remember how long the Haze lasts."

Torin nodded. "It is typically a week and a half, according to the reports, but it can depend on a lot of factors, like her diet and her general health. If this is the first time that she has been around any Alphas, I don't know how that may affect her. It could last longer, it could be shorter."

"So basically, you don't fucking know," Drocco snapped. "How long has she been in it so far?"

"Four days."

Four days out of a possible week and a half. So that left potentially...

Cailyn was turning around and sitting against the barrier, her back to him. Drocco frowned. That would not do.

"Drocco," Torin sighed.

Drocco growled at him. Torin needed to get the fuck out. The man was distracting him from his Omega.

"Will the barrier last longer than her Haze or not," he asked. "That's all I want to know, Torin. Can you tell me that, yes or no?"

Torin's gray gaze turned to steel. "You are the expert on Omegas," he said, his voice hard. "You told me to focus on my training and not study them, or spend my time concerned about their cycles or their Hazes or their breeding patterns. You learned all of that. So you need to focus and be the one to tell me if her Haze will last as long as the barrier. The barrier will end in eight days. If her Haze is typical, it will end in seven days. I cannot tell you if it's typical."

"Get out," Drocco ordered, as he headed toward the barrier to find a way for Cailyn to turn around.

Torin couldn't tell him what he needed to know. Drocco would simply have to wait and see.

That evening, Drocco pushed a jug of water at the barrier and watched as it penetrated and slid over to the other side. So the crafters were right. Cailyn sipped from it now and then but didn't seem to be eager to have it. She was more taken by the fact that Drocco was near the barrier.

Drocco began pushing through basins of soapy warm water, food, and other liquids she needed. She washed and sipped and nibbled, but Drocco got the feeling it was practiced behavior. He stopped trying to get her to take down the barrier. She simply hadn't been trained to listen to an Alpha during her Haze. In a way, it was encouraging. It suggested she hadn't been with an Alpha before. No real Alpha would allow an Omega to remain focused on her own needs during her Haze and not listen to him. He joined her masturbation, both of them watching the other pleasure themselves, both desiring the other through the glistening magic keeping them apart.

After a few days, Cailyn began to sleep a lot more than normal. Drocco noticed subtle changes in her behavior. She seemed more restless, not happy to simply lie around with her fingers in her pussy any longer. She also seemed to be noticing her surroundings more. She pushed out basins with dirty water and bowls of stale food, while looking around the room curiously, not just focused on Drocco.

It put him on edge. The barrier remained strong and if she was coming out of her Haze, she could potentially disappear through a portal.

At Torin's insistence, he had eaten a small plate of food each day from the day the Talent-crafters came, but he suspended all non-urgent visits to the room and began to focus all of his attention on everything she did. There were moments where she seemed unhappy, only to be taken over by the need to pleasure herself again. However, within two days, he noticed that the barrier seemed less solid than before. When he placed his hand on it, it gave under pressure. It was weakening. He issued an order for no one to enter, even Torin. He wanted no distractions and no chances for anything to go wrong. If the barrier weakened, he needed to be ready in case she tried to make use of the Talent. Clearly, she was very skilled and, although the Talent was not known for its combat uses, nothing would surprise him.

The day after he issued the order, the barrier began to shimmer. Drocco got up and stood next to it, watching and waiting. Cailyn lay asleep on the floor. She looked absolutely exhausted and Drocco clung to the hope that she would stay unconscious until the barrier dissolved.

The barrier glowed brighter and then completely disappeared.

A powerful wave of her magnificent scent slammed into Drocco, expanding to fill the entire room. It seemed to penetrate him and all thought left his mind, as his cock hardened even further.

He stood over the sleeping Omega and crouched down to her. Her dress, drenched in her own sweat, slick, and come, had managed to stay around her torso. Her hair was an absolute shaggy mess, tangled up and matted, but she was the most beautiful thing he had ever seen.

He ran his hands over her body, relishing the feel of her soft, smooth skin. He hooked his hand underneath her knees and spread her open, reaching in to feel that delicate, soft slit he had only ever seen through the barrier. It was dripping wet, an abundance of slick and come coating her entrance. He fumbled with his pants, releasing his hard cock that seemed bigger than he had ever felt it.

He pulled her toward him and lined himself up, rubbing the tip of his cock against her soft skin.

She moaned and fidgeted before her eyes fluttered open. He loomed over her, noticing her eyes weren't as gold as they were the day before. He pressed into her but couldn't get far. He pulled out slightly and pressed back in, a groan rumbling in his throat at how tight she was. She was coming out of her Haze and yet still opened her legs wider for him and whined as he pushed even further in.

"Take it, kitten," Drocco muttered, his breath jagged. "Take all of it."

She wriggled and ran a hand across his chest, mumbling something to herself that included the word "Alpha," her eyes half-lidded. He continued pressing forward, and she whimpered until he was all the way in. He forced himself to hold still to give her time to stretch for him. Her wriggling sparked incredible sensations that shot through his cock, and although a hot desperation rose to pound into her, he also wanted to savor the moment. He was the first Alpha to experience an Omega in the last one hundred and eleven years. Even in the midst of his rut, that thought seared through his mind.

He began to move slowly inside her, leaning his weight onto his hands either side of her head and grunting at the feel of her tight, wet slickness around him. Cailyn sucked in air and arched her back, her eyes rolling in her head as he sunk deeper, her whole body twitching underneath him. He worked in and out gradually getting faster as her slick gathered in a frothy mess at the base of his cock. She cried out, her pussy squeezing him as she grabbed his wrists and jerked her hips up to his, encasing him further. At that, he lost control. Twisting and jerking his hips, he slammed, and pounded, and drove into her furiously, intoxicated by her scent and the glorious feel of her. He reveled in all of her—her breathy moans, her fingers curling around his thick wrists, and the utter ecstasy on her face. He lost himself—so much so that when she screamed out in orgasmic bliss, her muscles contracting around him, he came so hard it overwhelmed him—his every pore so engulfed by uniquely delicious sensations and the potent scent of her that the orgasm tore through him, scratching out all thought from his head.

When he finally came back to his senses, he lay on top of her panting, crushing her into the ground as he still spurted inside her. He pushed up to his elbows and looked down at their joining. Her swollen, red pussy lips stretched around his knot—

the enlarged base of his cock—securely lodged inside her, locking them together.

Drocco had never been the type of Alpha that could knot with Betas. Grandfather had told him repeatedly that true Alphas only knotted with Omegas, and it seemed like that was true. The closest he'd gotten was a slight swelling with a Beta who had hidden that she was on a Haze recreator. He had never had a knot of this size and had never felt such pleasure at being encased so securely by a pussy so tight. He glanced up at Cailyn. She had fallen back asleep. He took a fistful of her hair, and let it run through his fingers. He licked her neck and sucked on it, enjoying the salty taste of her. He lifted her eyelids. The gold was almost gone. It was likely she would not be pregnant from this mating, and even though that was disappointing, it had to be done.

She became restless the longer the knot remained inside her, stretching her wide.

Winding a thick arm around her small waist, he carefully maneuvered them to an upright sitting position and lay her head on his chest, stroking her back until she settled.

Drocco stared down at her as she pressed her cheek to his chest. He had no idea who this woman was, where she came from, or what the hell she was doing in his palace, but her fate had been decided. She came to work for him under false pretenses, but it was clear that she was supposed to belong to him and there was no doubt now that she did. The problem was, she had revealed herself to be a traitorous deceiver. That had to be rectified immediately. He had to retrain her just for him and discover all the secrets that surrounded her existence. She would learn to be loyal and faithful to him—he would make sure of it.

CHAPTER EIGHT

CAILYN

Cailyn's consciousness returned in slow waves. Everything ached, and she groaned as the pain registered. She worked her jaw, trying to lubricate her dry mouth. Victoya should have been keeping her properly hydrated, but judging from her protesting limbs, it seemed the Haze had been more intense than normal this time.

Cailyn rolled over on the bed and cried out as a sharp, unfamiliar pain shot up between her legs. Her eyes flew open and she sat up carefully, her heart sinking as she looked around.

An enormous bed stretched all around her and at each corner, a thick bedpost rose up high to connect with a golden canopy overhead. Surrounding the bed was a lavish room. Thick, deep, umber carpet covered the floor and the walls were patterned with intricate decoration, color-coordinated in reds, browns, gold, and cream. Two burgundy couches sat on one side of the room, and next to them an engraved mahogany table with matching chairs.

Mats, rugs, and floor cushions littered one corner of the room, where a heavy dark curtain hung along one whole wall. Soft, ivory light poured from circular orbs in the ceiling and walls. Nothing looked familiar.

Cailyn tried to keep a hold of her panic. Moving slowly, she shifted to the edge of the bed and slipped her legs over the side. Pushing herself upright she stilled, thinking back to what she could remember. It took a few moments, as it always did, but soon the fragmented memories aligned in her mind.

Emperor Drocco.

She had created a barrier so he wouldn't get to her. She gritted her teeth. Judging by the pain between her legs, the fact she was naked, and the standard of the room around her, that had not worked. The barrier had been strong, created by his own blood. How the hell had he gotten through it?

She shook her head. That didn't matter right now. She had to get out immediately. Focusing her mind, she drew on the Talent to recreate her blocks. Nothing happened. She tried again, forcing her breathing to calm and her mind to clear. Nothing. She couldn't feel any magic in the air at all. Shit!

Pushing away the fear building in her, she got up and stumbled over to the wall-wide curtain. It couldn't be drawn; it seemed to be pinned in place at the top, but behind it was an enormous window that made up one whole side of the room, similar to the one in her quarters. The sunlight blinded her for a moment, but when her eyes adjusted she looked out upon a wide green forest, one she recognized. It surrounded a part of Lox Palace that no one had access to. It spread out far and wide before her, ending in the distance where it met with the city of Ashens.

A glass door in the center of the window led to a high-railed balcony, but of course, it was locked. She methodically searched the room high and low for a key or a way to escape, moving as quickly as she could while trying not to wince at the pain from her Haze.

At the compound, Omegas sometimes paired up to satisfy each other with their tongues and fingers and phallic contraptions, but Cailyn had never been interested in that. The idea of having to look another Omega in the eye afterward was too mortifying. Instead she and her friends, Victoya and Amara, would look out for each other on rotation, keeping each other safely in their rooms and making sure they drank, ate, and kept as clean as the Haze would allow. Some Omega spies would seek out men to have sex with while on their missions, to experience it so they could use it as part of their missions, but Cailyn never felt any need to do that. Besides, many of those spies ended up wanting it regularly, and she didn't become one of the best by seeking out such distractions. However, none of those Omegas she had spoken to about it had ever talked about being in such pain afterward.

Normally she would be achy after her Haze, but this time it felt like every muscle in her body had been stretched to its limit. She paused at the thought. Maybe they had. Cupping her sex, she gently felt along her sore slit, and a realization came to her. Drocco had knotted her—that's why she was so sore.

He could have mated her numerous times, which meant she could be pregnant.

She took a shaky breath and bit her lip as tears sprung to her eyes. No... she had to get a grip. Her memories of the Haze would come back soon enough and she would know for sure what had happened. For now, she needed to find a way out.

The enormous room had three doors; the thick and heavy one on the wall opposite the bed was locked from the outside, another was in a corner of the room and led to an equally lavish washroom that held small windows, and the last set of doors led to a wide closet that held a few sets of men's clothing.

Cailyn returned to the wall-length window and looked around for something to smash it. It was too thick to smash with her fist, but nothing in the room could be used for that purpose, there seemed to be a lack of ornamentation in general; no candlesticks, paintings or accessories—not even a clock. She paced the room, desperation overcoming her—there was no way out. Of course, Drocco would not allow the first Omega he had ever come across to escape so easily. He found a way to prevent her from using the Talent and was no doubt planning to keep her secure until he'd had his fill.

She was in the hands of the most vicious Alpha known to the Eastern Lands, who had an army of Alphas at his disposal. Her fate was bleak. She thought back to her home, the Omega Compound. All the warm, friendly Omegas that lived in peace and harmony. Her time with them was over—she would never see Victoya, or Amara, or the Mothers again. Her life would become exactly what she had been fighting to prevent all her life for Omegas. She dropped down against the wall next to the bed and dug her fingers into her palms as she blinked away angry tears.

As the raw edge of her anger faded, she calmed and tried to consider her situation logically. She always knew this outcome could be a possibility—all spies were told to prepare for it. She brushed her tears away and used the washroom, realizing that her hair had been washed and she had been cleaned up after her Haze. Maybe there was a servant she could appeal to. She returned to the bedroom and stripped a sheet from the bed to tie around herself and wait for the emperor, firming her mind. He could do whatever he wanted to her. She would never lead him to the Omegas.

When the lock turned in the heavy door opposite the bed, she stood and faced the door, her lips pressed into a straight line. Blurry memories of the Haze had returned and although she was glad he hadn't gotten through the barrier until the very end, an annoyance churned in her that he had fucked her when she had been mostly unconscious and exhausted.

The emperor's enormous bulk stepped through into the room, and the door closed immediately behind him, locking without him having to do anything. It confirmed her suspicions that guards stood outside the door.

Emperor Drocco looked as he always did—like a wild beast just barely contained in the flesh of an enormous man—but there was something fascinating about him that she hadn't noticed before.

That familiar nervousness bloomed immediately, trembling in her stomach along with a desire to go to him, but she knew it was because her blocks had gone. Without them, she wouldn't be able to resist his pheromones, but she would try.

The emperor looked around the room until he found her, his black eyes unreadable. "It is fortunate for you that you're finally awake."

"So you can knot me while I'm conscious this time?" Cailyn spat, instantly angry. "Yes, how fortunate for me."

He held her eyes for a moment, then turned slowly to place items she couldn't see on the table by the door, next to one of the sofas. "Your willful attitude was entertaining when I thought you were a Beta," he said casually, turning back to her. "When I thought I had to wait to fuck you. I'm not interested in being entertained by that now."

His calm manner disturbed her. "I was not aiming to entertain you."

"You were aiming to deceive me!" he bellowed suddenly.

Cailyn jumped but discarded her fear almost as soon as it rose.

The emperor's eyes blazed. "You are aware that I do not tolerate traitors?"

"I never swore loyalty to you."

The emperor thundered toward her, and Cailyn forced herself to hold her ground. He grabbed the sheet around her and ripped it away.

Cailyn didn't bother to react. She was barely holding out against the scent that swept in around her. Her nipples hardened and slick was already gathering between her legs, even though she was sore.

Drocco snarled as the last of the sheet left her. He grabbed her hair and yanked her head back, his face close to hers. "You lied constantly about who and what you are."

"And you raped me," she said evenly. "So I guess we are even."

His eyes narrowed. "Rape?" The distaste on his face surprised her somewhat. "You think you can plead to be fucked, offer me your pussy and your mouth for days, slam that tight hole up onto my knot and then cry rape?"

His words sent a tingly shiver down her spine and slick began to drip down her thighs, but her mind still worked, even if her body was lost to her. "That was hormones," she said, through gritted teeth. "Instincts and hormones. I wasn't sane or in my right mind."

Drocco made a noise of displeasure at the back of his throat. "Are you sane now?" His voice lowered. "Because I can smell the release of your slick and I haven't even touched you yet."

"Hormones," she said, breathier than she intended.

They glared at each other, a crackle of electricity shooting through Cailyn at the feel of his eyes roaming over her. His face contorted and he threw her by her hair onto the bed. She landed on her back and began to scramble away from him.

"Be still," he ordered.

She froze, and a part of her relaxed. It was easier on her emotionally to just follow his demands, but too much was at stake—she had to ignore the part of her that wanted to simply submit. Cailyn had never been one to take the easy route anyway.

"Open your legs," he demanded, undoing his pants.

Her legs were already half open before he finished speaking. She slammed them shut again, scrunching her lips together. All she had to do was focus.

Drocco's gaze intensified on her as he pulled off his shirt. "You fight your instincts."

She glared at him. She couldn't stop him from overpowering her, but she could try to make it as hard for him as possible. Since he wanted a submissive, it wouldn't please him.

However, once naked, the smell of him besieged her, making her almost dizzy with desire for him. His tanned bulk of a body was the epitome of a warrior— hard muscles bunched along his shoulders and down his arms, cut across his chest, his stomach— everywhere. Accompanying them were numerous scars that documented his success in battle, marking him a successful warrior. His cock stood up, a thick and long column jutted out for her. Memories of it inside her swam in her mind and a warmth agitated her body.

She wanted to be repulsed by everything about him—his rugged look, the potency of his Alpha stench, the violence signified by every mark on his body—but as an Omega, she had to appreciate that he was an incredibly handsome Alpha, and no amount of mental self-persuasion could convince her that his scent was anything other than enticingly delicious. Everything about him magnified her desire for him.

Drocco stroked himself, his enormous fist working up and down that magnificent cock, and a smirk spread slowly across his face.

Cailyn started, shocked as she realized she was somehow suddenly spread before him, her knees as far as they could go, her slick trickling onto the bed.

Drocco advanced, his black eyes triumphant. "Are you saying no, kitten?" he growled.

Cailyn swallowed the automatic answer that came to her lips, the one pushed forward by her Omega instincts to tell him to fuck and knot her until she was near enough blind. She cursed inwardly that she didn't even have the willpower to close her legs.

He stopped by the bed looking down at her, his eyes tracking down her body and all she could do was stare back. "Never cover yourself in this room," he ordered. "I want to see your body at all times."

She didn't answer and he reached for her, grabbing her hips and dragging her to the edge of the bed. She kept herself upright, her hands behind her to take her weight. She would not lie down before him.

"I'm sore," she said, evenly.

His eyes glittered. "I know."

Once her hips were at the edge, her legs still wide for him, Drocco ran a hand up across her stomach, over her breasts and pinched her nipples. She bit back a moan at the feel of his hands on her, sending goosebumps all over her. She gasped when he began tapping the head of his engorged cock on her clit. She melted into the sparks of sweet pleasure, sighing at the relief of not having to fight against her nature anymore.

"What is your name?" His voice was low.

"Cailyn."

"Cailyn what?"

She didn't say anything. She couldn't.

His mushroomed tip pressed against her bruised opening, and suddenly she was alert.

"What is your family name?" he asked.

"I don't know."

He pushed the tip in roughly, and she yelled, the raw pain dampening her pleasure. She seemed to be sore all the way inside.

"I don't know it," she shrieked. "I don't know it."

He paused, stilling his hips. "Are you a spy for King Malloron?"

"No," she breathed.

"Why are you here?"

"To look at your research."

"Why?"

Cailyn quickly gained control of herself before she opened her mouth again. She squeezed her eyes shut and clenched her jaw, fighting against her fear and impulses. She was not in the Haze. There was no excuse for answering his questions. She had just promised herself she would protect her people and she would stick by that—even if it meant sexual torture. She opened her eyes and looked upon the savage that had her at her most vulnerable. Regardless of his obvious allure, he was the enemy.

He seemed to sense the change in her and a fierceness entered his gaze.

He slammed into her pussy, a coarse grunt escaping him. She cried out as pain exploded up inside her. She tensed everything, intending to push him away. He moaned and grabbed her hair, pulling her head back so her chest jutted out as he slammed in again, and again, building a hard, steady rhythm.

Cailyn struggled against him for a moment before realizing the pain had dulled. In fact, it had blended with the harsh pleasure flooding her body. She breathed heavily as she stared up at the canopy, trying to figure out why the sensation of being filled so completely and so roughly caused such carnal satisfaction. When a warm mouth closed over her breast, and a rough tongue lapped her nipple, she stopped caring. The feeling overwhelmed and intoxicated her, and soon it wasn't enough.

Gripping Drocco's scarred, muscled arms, she flicked her hips every time he sunk in, fucking him back. A low growl built up in his chest and it sent tingles to every part of her body. She moaned with every pound that jolted her, the wet slaps of their mating filling her ears as her pleasure spiraled.

He sucked her nipple harder as his rhythm increased and by the time he licked up her neck, an orgasm crashed into her, seizing her whole body in an intense explosion of brilliant ecstasy.

As she recovered, Drocco's mouth pressed on her ear. "I haven't yet heard you say no, kitten," he sneered, before biting her earlobe. He hadn't even paused his thrusts while she came and still gripped her hair, holding her head tilted upward. As she blinked lazily at the canopy, the tremor of another orgasm coiled within her but before she could get there, he came, jerking into her with throaty grunts punctuating each jerk of his hips.

On his last thrust, his knot slammed in, stretching her wide as he spilled inside her. As they calmed, Drocco released her hair, and she lifted her head to find his eyes blazing into her. "Who sent you?"

She pressed her lips together, simply staring at him.

"Tell me who sent you," he ordered.

She looked away from him, toward the covered window.

Drocco placed his hands on her hips. He began to pull away from her, his knot pulling against the already sore muscles clamped onto it.

Cailyn snapped her head to look at him, her eyes wide in horror. "What the fuck are you doing?"

"Tell me who sent you," he said calmly, pausing his movement. "Why are you interested in my research? Where are the other Omegas?"

Cailyn's lip trembled, but she said nothing.

He moved again, pulling his hips back. "Last chance, kitten. Pick a question and answer it."

When she didn't answer, he began moving again.

Cailyn gritted her teeth as a severe pain tore into her, spreading from her pussy. She breathed deep, thinking of the compound as the pain turned excruciating. Then she began to scream. It was unlike anything she had experienced before and when she thought it couldn't get any worse, it hurdled to an extreme. He was ripping her apart!

"Tell me what I want to know," Drocco said, harshly.

She screamed uncontrollably, squeezing her eyes and fists tight as he slowly forced his knot all the way out of her. His semen gushed out after him, stinging like hell as it escaped.

She dropped onto the bed sobbing, reeling in agony and curled up on the bed trying not to move. She was sure she was torn and bleeding, but without the Talent, she couldn't heal.

Drocco moved around her, but she could barely register him. A dizziness swam in her mind and she felt close to passing out. After a few moments, he shifted her leg slightly, causing her to cry out. He pressed something cool on her pussy. Instantly the pain muted.

Cailyn froze, still sobbing while he applied whatever it was.

"Don't touch it," he said, before heading away from the bed. A moment afterward, the main door closed.

Lifting her leg, she looked down to see that he had smothered her in thick white cream that bubbled and fizzed on her skin. She couldn't see any blood, or the extent of the damage, but could guess how bad it was.

She dropped back into a tight curl and prayed he wouldn't fuck her again.

***

Of course, it was an unrealistic expectation. Within what felt like the next few hours he had returned and was rolling her onto her back.

Cailyn's eyes flew open, and she struggled against him, kicking and punching as hard as she could. It barely made any difference. He clasped her wrists in one of his hands and pressed them securely against her stomach. She still tried kicking him, but he grabbed her neck with his other hand, and she immediately went limp. The pressure at her neck felt oddly settling.

His face loomed over her, his black eyes gleaming with satisfaction. "So you are indeed able to submit like an Omega."

Cailyn snarled at him, but it took too much effort to maintain. And when he began rubbing her neck, a trickle of pleasure tingled down her spine. She sighed but resisted the urge to close her eyes and succumb to his touch. She stared at him, watching his eyes lower down her body. The hunger in his face, as well as his scent in the air, made her nipples harden.

He lowered and took one in his mouth as his hand around her neck continued its firm caress.

Cailyn tried to think about something else, but as his warm mouth worked one nipple and then the other, her arousal came over her so strongly, overwhelming her. He licked and sucked up her chest and down her stomach until the pungent aroma of her slick dominated the air between them. Drocco removed his hands from her neck, kneed her legs apart and slammed into her. She panted, shocked by the force of his thrusts as he yanked on her pinned wrists to pull her onto his cock as he built up another rough rhythm.

Of course, the stretch of being completely filled was even better than the first time. Cailyn didn't even know when he released her wrists, all she could do was accept the blissful, raw, delicious intensity that racked her body. Drocco groped and pinched her jolting body, squeezing her breasts and hips, sending her into a shuddering orgasm. He then grabbed her ass and lifted her up to drive into her with even more force. She came again before he did, thrusting his knot in and locking them together. As her breathing calmed, his questions began again. Cailyn suddenly realized she had felt no pain when he had entered her this time, even though he must have caused her damage before. She pondered on the thought as he continued to question her, purposefully blocking him out. The thick cream must have healed her. It hadn't seemed like a magical cream or potion—why hadn't she come across it before? When she didn't answer him, Drocco forced his knot out of her again, and the pain was just as brutal as the first time.

Drocco continued to fuck her, knot her, and tear her apart. He would treat her with the cream, which would repair her enough within a few hours so he could start all over again. He always used her Omega impulses against her, pinning her down and ensuring she was dripping and succumbing to whatever pleasure he roused. A few times, he didn't bother to pin her down—he let her try to fight him, a dark smirk on his face as he still touched and caressed her to an unavoidable arousal, and fucked her knowing she would fuck him back. Her orgasms, although powerful and consuming, became something to fear—something that also brought on powerful and consuming pain.

The emperor always questioned her before he started to rip her apart; where was she from, where did she grow up, where were all the Omegas, who sent her, why had she come, where was the real Miss Lefroy and her sister, who else in the palace knew about her, how did she learned the Talent...? She never answered any of it and he never failed to follow through with his threat and cause her as much pain as he could.

At varying intervals, he would order her over to the table next to the couch and push a bowl of spiced stew or fruity porridge toward her. He sat on the couch and watched her while she ate, the silence between them tense and uncomfortable. Cailyn always ate with the intention of keeping up her strength in case an opportunity to escape arrived, but with the constant pain she experienced, and the energy it took to resist him and her instincts, she began to lose interest in food. A few times when she didn't eat from the bowl he gave her, he would force feed her until the bowl was empty. It was unbearable and she quickly decided to just eat to prevent the experience.

At first, she kept track of the days by hobbling over to peek behind the heavy drape when he wasn't in the room to see when night fell, but she couldn't always make it over there and soon the hours and days blurred into each other.

Drocco seemed to leave at random times, usually after he had applied the healing cream. Whenever he wasn't in the room, Cailyn pulled all the sheets and duvets off the bed to lie down in the corner where all the mats and floor cushions were. She found she slept better rolled up in the sheets and blankets, as far away as possible from the bed where he tortured her with pleasure and pain multiple times every day. Whenever he re-entered the room, he redressed the bed with new sheets before dragging her back to it and starting all over again.

After a while, a deep ache grew in her pelvis. As it became stronger, it hurt to walk, and she was in constant agony. Drocco stopped fucking her, only to continue torturing her by simply flicking a finger into her hip every time she didn't answer a question, causing a brutal pain to ricochet down her legs. When she healed enough for her pelvis to stop hurting, he began fucking her again. Soon Cailyn lost all sense of time and began to despair at what her life had become—pleasure, pain, and loneliness.

"This can stop whenever you'd like," Drocco huffed one day, as he dragged her back to the bed. "When you feel like you would like to act like a real Omega, then this will stop."

"I am a real Omega," Cailyn snapped at him. She was almost completely healed but knew she wouldn't be once he'd finished with her.

"You are not," Drocco bit out, throwing her onto the bed. "You are defiant and disobedient, you have no desire to please me. You are nothing like an Omega should be."

"And how would you know what a real Omega is?" Cailyn hissed, sitting up and glaring at him. "You have never met an Omega. All you have are old, traditionalist, outdated ideals, probably from some old abusive Alpha who would destroy and kill Omegas for his own entertainment."

Drocco visibly bristled. "Alphas do not kill Omegas; it is Betas who are at fault for that."

"Betas have never had any reason to kill Omegas. It is Alphas who take their pleasure however they want."

Drocco snarled at her. "Alphas have no reason to take anything, Omegas willingly give."

"I have not willingly given you anything," Cailyn said, her eyes blazing. "You take it anyway."

"Are you saying you do not give yourself to me?" Drocco asked, his tone dangerous. "Are you saying I am misreading your scent, and your slick, and your greedy little thrusts to fuck me harder?"

"I don't give myself only to be tortured," Cailyn said, sharply. "You think a Beta would do that?"

Drocco's nostrils flared, but she was too angry to register the sign.

"You think Betas could have destroyed Omegas to the death rate recorded over a hundred years ago while Alphas sat back and did nothing? Do you think Alphas would have let Betas destroy their fuck toys? No. It was the Alphas killing us. Betas couldn't stop them."

"No!" Drocco bellowed. "You lie. All Alphas cherished their Omegas. They viewed them as precious and something to be looked after and cared for. You are twisting it because you're a fucking spy!"

Cailyn shifted herself so she was sitting with her legs in front of her. "All right. If that's true, continue to *cherish* me, Emperor," she said, spreading her legs open wide. "Have me come on your knot only to rip me open. Oh, how lucky I am to be cared for!"

Drocco exploded in anger. His roar shuddered through her, and she jumped as he grabbed at the sheets and duvet to get to her. She scrambled backward but he caught her leg and dragged her to him. Flipping her around he pressed her head into the bed and lifted up her hips, propping her on her knees.

"Do you think this couldn't be worse, kitten?" he boomed. He ran the tip of his cock along her ass crack.

She gasped into the bed and fought against him trying to escape, but he held her too tightly.

"Do you think I wouldn't fuck you here," he said, pressing his massive cock on her asshole, "and knot you? How do you think your ass would feel if I tore that open repeatedly? And then tore open your pussy?"

"No," Cailyn yelled, her voice muffled into the bed. True fear bloomed in her for the first time. Omega females were not made for penetration in their asses like Omega males. Many of the deaths reported sodomization as the starting point for unrecoverable internal trauma and infection in her kind. Maybe not if it had been Betas, but Alphas were huge and Drocco was larger than most. She wouldn't survive it. "No, please don't!"

"I have no incentive to stop," Drocco threatened, his tip pressing harder until it entered.

Cailyn cried out, thrashing against him but unable to escape the new pain piercing her.

"Tell me what I want to know!"

"I'm from the Eastern Lands," Cailyn blurted out. She began to cry. "I grew up in Cillford. My family were farmers who worked on the land, but I don't remember them."

The Alpha holding her in place was silent for a moment. "The Omegas?"

"They're safe. And mostly together. They were not taken. They chose to leave society." Cailyn sobbed harder at what she had just revealed. No one—absolutely no one alive who wasn't an Omega—knew that information. And she had just given it to the worst Alpha known to the Eastern Lands.

"Why?"

Sobbing so hard with her face pressed into the bed made it difficult for Cailyn to answer. "Abusive Alphas" was all she could manage.

Drocco yanked her head to the side. "Stop crying!"

She pressed her mouth closed and tried to stop, her body jerking as she wept.

"How were the Alphas abusive?"

"They would fuck and knot girls of twelve who's dynamic had only just been discovered," she stuttered out, heaving. "Most of the girls died from internal bleeding and rough treatment. The Alphas would also share an Omega in her Haze with multiple Alphas. Over time, these Omegas became shells of what they once were, used only for breeding and abuse. Many of them started to die in childbirth—the child would not survive either. This treatment was widespread across all the known Lands. The entire Omega population was under threat. They chose to leave."

When she finished speaking there was a silence.

Drocco pulled his tip out and his hands left her. She curled up onto the bed, sobbing with her head tucked into her chest. After a few long moments, the door shut.

When the door opened again, Cailyn was curled up surrounded by her stack of sheets and duvets in the corner. A dark depression had taken hold of her and she had cried until she could no longer squeeze out another tear. After all of her righteous intentions, she had told the enemy sacred information at the first sign of real permanent damage to herself. What kind of spy was she? What had happened to all her training, all the accolades of her achievements for the hidden Omega population? She was the first Omega to reveal them. That's what she was. That's what she'll be remembered for, if there was anyone left to remember her by the time Drocco finished with them.

She listened, waiting for Drocco's wide hand to reach into the blankets surrounding her and pull her out. There was shuffling, and then nothing. She waited, breathing shallowly. Drocco never made much noise when he walked on the thick carpet. He could be a foot away from her, waiting to yank her out and she wouldn't know it.

After the silence stretched longer than she could bear, she peeked out of her cocoon. The room seemed empty. Her eyes swept the room again, and she noticed the enormous mass on the bed. Surprised, she lifted the sheet over her head and slowly climbed out, wincing at the pain that still hurt her ass. Drocco lay on the bed, his breathing steady, and as she stepped closer she realized his eyes were closed. He was sleeping.

For a moment, she didn't know what to do, and then her training kicked in. She tiptoed to the door trying it, but of course, it was locked. She checked the clothes he had discarded by the bed, but they held no keys or any useful items of any kind. On the table was only a few tubs of the cream he used regularly to heal her but nothing else. She continued to tiptoe around the room, checking if anything had changed that would allow her to escape, but nothing had. There was still no way out.

She stood staring at him lying peacefully, wondering if there was a way to kill him to ensure his death. But without the Talent, and without her blocks, she was useless. If she tried and failed, her life would be even more unbearable, and if she succeeded, how would she get out of the palace? A plan like that required careful thought. She didn't even know for certain that he was the reason she couldn't use the Talent—something else could be wrong. What if she managed to escape and still didn't have the Talent? Every Alpha she came into contact with would smell her. The good thing was, if he was now sleeping in the room, it gave her options to find a way to kill him or escape in the future.

She crept back to her makeshift bed and settled in. It took her a while to get to sleep with him in the room, but eventually, exhaustion overcame her.

When she woke, Drocco had gone. She slept again, this time more peacefully now that he wasn't in the room. When she woke again, a platter of food sat on the table by the door, but Drocco wasn't there.

He didn't return for hours and a nervousness crept over her about his absence. What if he was mobilizing his army to seek out the Omegas? What if he was sourcing some kind of torturous equipment to use on her? She just didn't know.

Long hours seemed to pass by. Food and water appeared on the table when she slept, but Drocco didn't return. The depression around her situation pressed in on her, and she began to wonder if she had become more of a liability to her people than a help. There was a protocol that would allow an Omega to kill herself if the situation became dire—Cailyn considered whether she had arrived at that point. Suicide was deemed a highly heinous act considering how precious every single Omega life was. However, if she was endangering them all, then the protocol had to apply, didn't it? She'd once been sure she could eventually find a way out, but what if she didn't? She had already revealed information she shouldn't have. However, after surveying the room, there seemed to be nothing that would help her to complete that task anyway. Even the sheets she slept in could not be tied to anything to make a noose. Her head spinning, she lay down to sleep.

She woke to a hand gripping her calf and dragging her out of her cocoon of sheets. Drocco lifted her up and carried her to the bed.

She lay there, her depression seeping into her even further as she realized that her suffering had not yet ended. She had fully healed now, but wouldn't remain so for long.

Drocco leaned over her, his hands on either side of her, caging her in. She didn't look up at him, keeping her head turned to one side. His scent surrounded her, drawing forth that damn slick. Her body worked against her at every turn. She never thought that she would hate being an Omega, but her reaction to her captor was ridiculous. She now had a first-hand understanding of why the Mothers had removed themselves and all other Omegas from the main population. Alphas were sick fucking bastards, and Omegas were attracted to them nonetheless.

Drocco dropped onto his elbows and pressed his nose into the crook of her neck. He took a breath in and ran his nose up to a spot behind her ear. Cailyn frowned at the action. He had never started that way before. When he licked her there, dragging his teeth over the skin, she couldn't help but shiver.

He took his time to kiss and lick her all the way down to her breasts. Taking a nipple in his mouth, he sucked and nibbled until she gasped, her pussy clenching as the pleasure fluttered through her. He moved to the other, running his rough palm over her stomach and tugging on the nipple he had just released. As he became rougher, pleasure zinged through her every pore, and she surrendered to the feeling, eager to escape her depression. If she could discard the guilt, even for just a few moments, she would take it. The pain would no doubt come later, but for now, she would enjoy what she could.

Drocco ran his hands across her body, pressing his fingers into her limbs, massaging them and relieving stress that she didn't even know she had. His fingers slipped between her legs and he pressed them into her drenched slit, rubbing circles over her clit.

Cailyn moaned, rotating her hips to meet his fingers.

His mouth made its way down her stomach to her mound, where he licked and sucked before his tongue dipped into her slit. He took his time running his tongue along her lips, groaning into her like a man savoring a rare delicacy. She tried to ignore him as best she could, but every sound that came out of him turned her on and heightened her pleasure. He licked and sucked every area of her pussy and then zeroed in on her clit, dragging his tongue across it and flicking her gently. She ground her hips into his face as he suckled on her, his tongue dabbing and swirling in the most delicious ways as her orgasm rose rapidly. When she came, he held her hips as she bucked against him, keeping his mouth on her until she calmed, her clit throbbing.

"You're so sexy." Drocco's mouth hovered above her pussy, shining with her fluids. His liquid black eyes were on her as he spoke, low and raspy. "I have never seen anything like it, kitten."

As soon as he spoke, Cailyn froze. Her high was fading away, the reality of her situation returning. He never made her come without also giving her pain.

He stood up and she watched him as she lay there, through lidded eyes, for what he was going to do next. His trousers tented at his crotch, but he never made to remove them.

He looked down at her for a long moment and then turned toward the table. "Come and eat," he ordered.

For the next stretch of time, a new pattern emerged. Twice a day, Drocco would leave the room. On his return, he would feast on her body until she came in his mouth, and then watch her eat at the table. Cailyn tried to remain alert. Something about his behavior wasn't right. He didn't seem to want to gratify himself, after so many days of fucking her. Part of her, that stupid Omega impulse part of her, was annoyed by this, while the more logical side of her was glad that he kept his cock far away from her pussy.

Eventually, though, her impulses began to strengthen. She caught herself wondering what was wrong with her—why this perfect Alpha didn't want to mate with her anymore. Furthermore, she was becoming more and more unsatisfied with just his mouth. Of course, the orgasms were incredible. But now that she had experienced being filled and stretched wide by his cock and knot, a large part of her wanted it, even though he had been abusing her with it. Maybe she was crazy, or developing some kind of distorted need for him that captives tended to develop after being with their abusers for so long.

And why hadn't he continued questioning her? She had given him information that had surely piqued his curiosity. She hadn't even answered his question about where the Omegas were located, and yet he didn't continue to try and find out anything else. It confused her. What did he want? She did not ask him, in case he went back to torturing her. And she had no idea what she would do if he did. If he threatened to sodomize her again, she couldn't guarantee that she wouldn't speak. She was a coward. She had to accept that. She had been trained not to fear her own death, but the training that was supposed to help her face certain types of torture had been ineffective.

The more she considered it, the more she realized that she should be more focused on finding a way to kill herself. Now was the perfect time. Drocco only knew so much, but he didn't know enough to actually find the Omegas. She had told the Mothers in the note she had sent along with her findings that she would be taking a short break in Ricsdale before checking in with them again. Eventually, they would realize that she had been compromised and that everything that she knew could be told to the emperor. They would have to take precautions. But it would be better if the emperor didn't actually know much, and she had to ensure that he didn't force her into telling him any more.

One day, after Drocco had left, she tried to pull down the drapes across the window. She pulled and yanked them, but they held fast. She picked up a chair from the table and swung it against the glass, but even though the chair was solid wood it did not break the window. She tried everything she could but nothing worked. She began punching the window as her anger and desperation reached its peak. She smashed her fist against it over and over, screaming with frustration that she had been stuck in this room for days on end. It was only when she saw blood on the glass that she realized that she was damaging herself.

Cradling her hand and feeling desperately sorry for herself, she crawled into her sheets and cried herself to sleep.

When Drocco returned and pulled her out of her sleeping place, he was furious.

"What the fuck did you think you were doing?" he bellowed, his entire body twitching with anger. "Do you think you can get through that glass? Do you think you're going to get out of here unless I allow it? You will never leave, kitten. No one enters this room but me, and no one will leave this room but me."

Cailyn frowned, suddenly realizing something. "What about the servant that washed my hair and cleaned me up after my Haze?"

"I did that," Drocco said, glaring at her. "So if you're hoping for someone to come in and save you, don't waste your energy."

Cailyn didn't say anything. She barely looked at him as he continued yelling at her. It didn't matter what he said. She would keep trying to find a way to escape or kill herself, whichever option presented itself first. He applied the cream to her hand and bandaged it up.

Sometime later, while she ate at the table, Drocco began speaking unexpectedly.

"When is your next Haze?" he asked, from the couch where he watched her.

Cailyn hesitated at the sudden question. "What?"

"When is your next Haze?"

Cailyn frowned. "I don't know. I don't know how long ago the last one was. I can't tell time in this room."

"How regularly do you normally have it?"

Cailyn shrugged. "It is irregular."

Drocco leaned towards her. "I will caution you about lying to me, kitten. I know that Omegas are very regular with their Haze. Some as frequent as fortnightly, others every six months, but always regular."

Cailyn shot him a hard look. "I have been suppressing my Omega impulses with the Talent for years. My Haze has never been regular."

Drocco got up, cursing furiously. "Why would you do that? Is spying so important to you that you would damage yourself for it?"

"I'm not damaging myself," Cailyn said, her voice low.

"Of course you are! The Haze is a natural part of your cycle. No wonder you are so disobedient, you are completely destroying your natural Omega impulses."

Cailyn shrugged. There was no point arguing with him. The man seemed to think that he knew everything about Omegas, even though he had no recent information. He wouldn't believe anything she said so there was no point in even conversing with him. Her energy was better spent trying to find a way out.

"It is likely that you went into your Haze because of Alpha pheromones," Drocco said, thoughtfully. "Maybe in the presence of your Alpha, your Haze will become more regular."

Cailyn snorted. "My Alpha? Do you intend to spread me around your army until you find him?"

Drocco stopped pacing and turned to her slowly. "I will not be sharing you with anyone."

Cailyn frowned. "So what are you talking about? Who is my Alpha?"

Drocco leaned over her, one hand on the back of her chair and the other on the table, his face close to hers. "*I* am your fucking Alpha."

Cailyn's eyes narrowed. "You are not. "

Drocco tensed. "What?"

"You're not my Alpha!"

"Oh, I'm not?" Drocco straightened, looking down at her, the hint of a smirk on his face.

Cailyn glared at him. "Do you think you own me?"

Drocco grabbed her arm and pulled her up from the table. "Of course I own you, kitten." He laughed. "Your naiveté is almost as sexy as your pointless attempts to avoid arousal."

Cailyn gritted her teeth. He still thought of her as a plaything, a toy, a kitten. She thought she was his prisoner but it was much worse, of course. She tried to think of something to snap at him, but he was already lifting her up and carrying her to the bed.

"Do you really believe you don't belong to me?" he asked, chuckling under his breath as he lay her down.

"Physically imprisoning me is not the same as being my Alpha, Emperor," Cailyn said, hotly. "You know an Omega gets to choose her bonded mate. I have to willingly give that title. You cannot just claim it!"

"Then tell me I'm your Alpha," he said, his voice suddenly hard.

"You are not!"

His eyes narrowed. "Tell me!"

"No!" It was the only bit of control Omegas had. She would not give it up—she did not care what he did. He lifted her arms above her head and clasped her wrists together in one hand. A twinge of panic coiled in Cailyn's stomach at the sudden restraint but she kept her mouth shut.

Drocco lowered to kiss her neck and she shivered, goosebumps prickling over her whole body as she breathed him in. He bit the base of her neck and licked across her chest and down between her breasts.

"You think I am not your Alpha?" he murmured. He captured a nipple in his mouth and sucked, working it hard with his mouth as his rough tongue brushed it.

Cailyn moaned and arched her chest up to him, her whole body tingling.

He released her breast with a pop and nibbled down her stomach. "That feeling," he said, "is your body reacting to your Alpha, kitten."

Cailyn mumbled but he was already pressing his face into her sex, breathing her in.

"You smell so good," he mumbled. He licked the length of her slit slowly. "Your pussy belongs to me, your slick comes to me when I want it, every inch of this incredible body is mine." He suckled her clit, releasing her wrists and positioning himself between her legs.

Cailyn watched him, becoming drunk on the high he always caused.

He lifted his head. "Tell me I am your Alpha."

"No," she breathed.

"No?" He dipped his tongue back to her pussy and pushed it into her.

Cailyn whined and rotated her hips. It was the first penetration she'd had in a long time, and she realized that she'd always craved it. And then it was gone.

She glanced down, annoyed. Drocco had lifted his head and was looking at her.

"I am your Alpha. Say it."

Cailyn tucked her feet under her hips and lifted them, rising up to his mouth. Drocco laughed.

He leaned in and sucked her, his eyes alive with mirth.

Cailyn whimpered, spreading her knees wider as her orgasm approached. The man surely had a talented tongue.

Then he stopped again. "Tell me I am your Alpha, kitten."

Cailyn cursed, a sudden anger gripping her at his lack of attention to her pussy. "Why do you want me to say it? You despise me! Why would you want me to be your bonded mate?"

Drocco's head tilted. "You think I despise you?"

"It is well-known you hate spies and you hate the Talent," Cailyn responded, dropping her hips back to the bed. "You are only enamored with me because I am an Omega. It doesn't make us bonded mates."

"You don't think I wanted to fuck you before I knew you were an Omega?" Drocco asked.

"Of course you did. You fuck every female you come across. That is well-known too."

Drocco's grin widened. "Does that annoy you, kitten?"

"Of course not," Cailyn snapped, though a wild anger swept through her. "It is just yet another example of why we cannot be bonded mates."

Drocco lifted his chin. "Why?"

"You are insatiable. And when you get bored, you discard the women you have been with to find another. The man I would choose for my Alpha would not behave that way. He wouldn't abuse me the way that you do. My Alpha is still somewhere out there; you are not him."

Drocco growled, and the sound vibrated through her body. "You have driven me to treat you the way I have," Drocco said harshly. "It will not always be like this. You already know my opinion about Omegas and the Alpha/Omega connection."

"Yes. You believe your Omega should serve you." Cailyn said, her dark mood beginning to deepen. "You believe you are justified in that thought because you can physically dominate any Omega that disobeys you." She looked up at him. "You know nothing about real Omegas, Emperor. You think we are all virginal submissives with no thoughts in our heads other than to breed for Alphas."

Drocco stilled. "Were you not a virgin?"

Cailyn almost rolled her eyes. That was the only thing he seemed to have heard. It was hopeless talking to him. "Does it matter?" she said, shrugging and sitting up.

"Yes," Drocco barked. "How many men have you fucked?"

"How many women have you fucked?" she shot back, tired of his demands. For a moment it had seemed he was capable of having a real conversation with her, and then suddenly it had turned into a display of his domination and ego.

"Don't play with me, kitten," Drocco said, his fists clenching. "I want to know who has been with you. Their names and locations."

He seemed to think they were destined to be some kind of great love, destined to be mates, even though she was his prisoner. Surely he couldn't be that deluded. Cailyn glared at him, her fury rising. Maybe she needed to strongly discourage him. "There have been many, many men before you. And there will be many men after you. I will fuck every single Alpha and Beta I find, and I'll love it, Emperor. You and your cock will be a distant memory and I'll never give you another thought because you are not my Alpha!"

A tight pressure locked around her neck, and a hard jolt hit her back before she could register what had happened. Drocco's face swam in front of her. She had somehow moved from the bed to against the wall and his enormous hand pressed in around her neck pinning her to it.

"I'm the only man you will ever fuck from this moment on!" Drocco roared. "I will not share you. Ever! You will never have an opportunity to fuck anyone else." His hand tightened around her neck as he leaned in, growling. "No other man alive should have had what I own. You will tell me who they are

136

and where they are, and then you *will* declare me your Alpha!"

A pressure built up in Cailyn's head and she began to feel light-headed. She fought against him for a moment before realizing he was strangling her. This was her way out. It was the perfect solution.

She dropped her hands to her sides as the uncomfortable feeling turned unbearable. Her ears began to ring, and she couldn't hear anything he said but he still ranted in a vicious fury. She watched him, unable to help admiring the complete, fierce, beauty that he was, as everything fell dark.

CHAPTER NINE

DROCCO

Drocco stormed into the training grounds in a frenzy. He had almost killed her. His own future mate! She had infuriated him to the point of such anger, he had forgotten his own strength. She was so small; she wouldn't have survived if he had squeezed her throat much longer.

He grabbed his double-ended, multi-blade sword and his favorite double-sided battle axe before heading toward the grounds.

The healer that had examined and treated her said she would recover to full strength within a few hours with treatment, sleep, and minimal distress, but that didn't appease him. He had caused it, and the idea of that cut him deep. He had lost control, which he hated, and nearly lost the one thing he was desperate to keep. What if he did it again?

Torin saw him coming and quickly sent the warriors he was training away before Drocco arrived.

"No, Drocco," he called as he approached. "They are here for training, not for you to take your frustrations out on them again."

Drocco roared and swung his axe. It dropped with a heavy clang on Torin's shield.

Torin darted back. "Drocco! Calm down."

"I want to train!" Drocco bellowed, twisting his sword above his head before slicing it toward Torin. Torin danced out of the way, spun around, and jabbed at Drocco with his sword. Drocco dodged and parried with his sword.

"Stop, Drocco," Torin said, harshly. "You have no shield and you are too angry for training."

"I am the emperor, I train whenever I want!"

"Yes, you are the emperor." Torin lowered his shield and his sword, leaving himself dangerously vulnerable. "Do you want your men to see you like this? You want them to see you so out of control after all the success you have achieved for finding an Omega?"

Drocco froze, his chest heaving. Out of the corner of his eye, he could see the warriors Torin had sent off gathering at the edge of the grounds.

The entire Empire had rejoiced upon hearing that Drocco had an Omega in the palace. Many had detected Cailyn's scent lingering in the Great Hall, and more had reveled in her scent after she had been taken from the office where she'd had her Haze. The word had spread quickly, and soon many territories and cities that had been previously reluctant to join the Lox, were swearing fealty, sending the heads of their family members as proof of their loyalty.

Drocco had kept up the pretense—boasting in the triumph and celebrations like he was supposed to, but he and Torin knew the truth. Finding the Omega had been luck, and in fact, she had tricked him for a long time. He had been furious that she had been right under his nose, even as he had berated his warriors about being vigilant for spies. His anger had fueled his main goal, which was to get Cailyn to tell him where the other Omegas were. After that— after she had been through the appropriate punishment—they could start their real relationship. However, nothing with Cailyn had gone how he had expected it.

"You're not on the same kind of battlefield anymore, Drocco," Torin said, after a long moment of silence. "This political battlefield is all about image and perception. Everything you do will be watched, and your army has expectations of you."

Drocco growled in the back of his throat. "My army has no right or inclination to question anything I do."

"You promised them Omegas," Torin said. "Now you have one for yourself."

"So you're saying they are angry that I benefit and they don't?"

"No, they are encouraged by this and happy for you," Torin insisted. "But eventually they will want your success to lead to their own." Torin eyed him. "This isn't the first time you have come from your bedroom furious and ready for blood. If it becomes clear that you cannot handle her, word will spread. You will lose some of your warriors." His voice lowered. "If you are having trouble with the Omega, you can assign someone else to break her."

"No one touches my mate," Drocco thundered.

Torin stared at him, shock in his eyes. "You are claiming this one as your mate?"

"Of course I am."

"I didn't realize," Torin muttered. He glanced away and then peered back at Drocco. "You realize that as a spy and a Talent-crafter she is everything the Lox despise—"

"Torin," Drocco said, a clear warning in his tone. This was exactly the same vein of conversation he had just had with Cailyn.

"I'm just saying you don't need to select the first one—"

Drocco swung his sword so quick, Torin barely had time to react. Even though he jerked backward, the tip caught his chin. The Beta stumbled back and the warriors at the edge of the grounds started in surprise.

"She is my mate," Drocco growled, as Torin cradled his chin. "I have been sure since I first scented her, perhaps even before then. You will never discuss this with me again. Understood?"

Torin nodded, a stunned curiosity in his eyes as blood dripped between his fingers.

Drocco glared at him, his fingers twitching on his sword handle. Cailyn had looked upon Torin twice—one of those times while in her Haze. Was he the kind of man she would seek to fuck? A man he could cut down easily before she could even make that choice?

Drocco caught his train of thought and threw down his weapons before he could do anything stupid.

"May I make a suggestion, Drocco?" Torin asked, quietly.

Drocco grunted his consent.

"It has been a while since you looked at your reports. There may be something you have forgotten about Omegas that would help you."

Drocco exhaled as he thought. An idea formed in his mind and he dipped his head in a sharp nod and glanced at the warriors. "Carry on."

Drocco headed straight to his carriage house and told them to prepare to leave immediately. He sat and waited as they rushed about, a deep agitation within him about what he had almost done to Cailyn. Much of it was because she fought so hard against her instincts. It was almost as if she didn't want to bond with him, and the thought of that angered him even more. Her body and her responses to him during their mating told a completely different tale; however, even though there were moments when she seemed like she was settling, she was simply distant. Her mind was somewhere else and not focused on him. It was displeasing.

As a spy, she should surely realize he had to torture her to get information. He had to break her, and he had to do it with his knot. That was the trick to breaking a prisoner—enforcing pain on the one thing that made them who and what they were. Omegas were the only dynamic that could be truly knotted, and so that was where Cailyn had to suffer. Of course, it didn't help that it had to happen after he fucked her. Her body was exquisite in every way, her sweet, dripping pussy was made for him, and yet neither of them could fully enjoy the experience past their base needs. When she orgasmed now, it was nothing like the beauty of the first time because she knew what was coming next. It tainted their mating, and that was even more of a reason to get the information out of her so they could move on.

It didn't sit well with him when she cried. In fact, he fucking hated it. It wasn't as if he hadn't been in utter agony too every time he had to pull out of her. But he had made sure he fully lathered her in the healing cream before he left to treat himself. If he hadn't been sure it would repair her completely, he would've had to find a different method to break her.

He had been surprised at how resilient she had been, proud of her even. He had only made her come in his mouth that first time as a reward for holding out so long to give him that information, but then he found he couldn't stop sucking her. It was the only time she was unreserved and without fear. It was the only time she had touched him outside of her Haze—gripping his hair and scratching his scalp. He loved the way she writhed and wriggled, the way she spread her legs and humped her hips so nastily to feed him, not even to mention how good she tasted. He couldn't get enough. When that unique blend of her slick and come saturated his face, dominating his every inhale... nothing else was important. He had suspended the interrogation so that could continue for a little while. He hadn't even fucked her, even though the desperation rose violently every time.

"We are ready, your Imperial Majesty," muttered his driver, bowing low before him.

Drocco climbed into his carriage instructing them to head to the Records Keep. Torin's suggestion had been reasonable but not if he was to believe Cailyn. Much of what she had said about how Omegas had been treated had been left out of all the reports he read. Even his grandfather hadn't mentioned it, and he had been a ferocious Alpha who had deeply loved his Omega. If Omegas were responsible for their own disappearance, it changed everything. If they hated Alphas and didn't want Alphas in their lives, that presented a problem on a level that he had not been prepared for. After she had revealed that, he had scoured every piece of information his grandfather and father had left him. There had been subtle hints, but nothing definitive. What if Cailyn was the one mistaken? What if her capturers had brainwashed her? How could he know what information to believe? Regardless of her belief of the Omegas torturous existence before their disappearance, he couldn't discount every single record. He needed further information.

He stared out of the window, wondering if something was wrong with Cailyn that his healer couldn't see. She was certainly an Omega by all physical accounts, but he couldn't understand why she was so headstrong. Maybe the blocks had had a lasting damaging effect on her personality. He needed to know more.

The clerks and keepers gathered at the entrance of the Keep to applaud and cheer him when he arrived.

Drocco strode straight to the head keeper, who began gushing at him immediately. "Congratulations, your Imperial—"

"I need a private word with whichever keeper is most knowledgeable about Omegas and the Alpha/Omega connection."

The head keeper nodded graciously. "That is myself, your Imperial Majesty. Please follow me."

He led Drocco through the Keep, the clerks still applauding, only stopping to bow as Drocco passed. The keeper led him up a smaller staircase near the back of the first floor to a bare room that held only a table, two chairs and a wide window on one of the walls. His guards waited outside when he entered.

"This room is private?" Drocco asked, looking around.

The keeper nodded. "Nothing said in this room can be heard elsewhere, your Imperial Majesty. It's one we use for the reporting of sensitive information."

Drocco eyed him for a moment. He would have rather spoken to a man he could kill after to protect the information he was about to disclose, but the head keeper seemed too useful. He would have to be careful. Finally, he nodded.

The head keeper smiled at him. "What can I help you with?"

"I need to know how to correct Omega behavior to its original and traditional state."

The keeper frowned in confusion. "Correct Omega behavior?"

"Yes, so she is submissive and eager to please."

"There are no such correction methods recorded, Emperor."

Drocco exhaled and began pacing the small room. "How does an Alpha keep his Omega from being willful and disobedient?"

The keeper's frown deepened. "The Alpha/Omega connection is known to be a mutual one. Omegas have no reason to reject it." He hesitated. "Is your Omega being... uncooperative?"

"Yes," Drocco bit out. "She refuses to reveal the locations of the other Omegas."

The head keeper nodded. "Maybe she doesn't know."

"Possibly," Drocco said, unwilling to reveal what Cailyn had told him.

"Tell me about how she behaves," the keeper asked. "Does she talk to you about anything else?"

"No."

"Do you... mate?"

Drocco narrowed his eyes at the man. "What kind of question is that? Of course we fuck."

"No offense, your Imperial Majesty, I'm just trying to ascertain her mood," the keeper said, gently. "Is she happy to have been found?"

"No."

When Drocco didn't elaborate, the head keeper took a moment to think. "What is her opinion of you?"

"Not good. She is very resistant to me. She fights against her urges to mate and tells me I am not her Alpha." A twinge of anger stirred in him at the thought of her rejection.

"She doesn't want you as her Alpha?" the head keeper asked, shocked.

"She doesn't know what she wants," Drocco said, harshly. "Her body tells me one thing, her mouth tells me another. I can actually see the physical strain on her when she opposes me, yet she still does it. Frequently. She will not accept the truth of what is natural to her." He looked at the keeper. "Is it true that she cannot be forced to soul-bond?"

"Yes. It is well recorded that Alphas who try to bond with an Omega without her reciprocating, suffer an unpleasant existence until they die. The soul-bond has to be mutual—the claiming bites should happen at the same time, or at least the Omega's bite should happen first."

Drocco exhaled harshly. He had hoped that piece of information was incorrect. "What kind of unpleasantness do the Alphas experience?"

"They become a victim to their Omega's emotions," the keeper explained. "And, since Alphas are not supposed to be overwhelmed by such emotions, it distorts their outlook and they become tormented."

"Fuck," Drocco muttered.

"Over time, they become crazy. Their lifespan is drastically shortened and they lose their sense of everything that makes them an Alpha."

"Does the same thing happen in reverse?"

"No," the keeper said, shaking his head. "Omegas can deal better with the Alpha's emotions, though it is more satisfying for both if he returns the bite."

A silence fell over the room as Drocco considered what the keeper said. Biting Cailyn first was completely out of the question. He had to make her bite him first. "What about in her Haze? Will an Omega soul-bond during her Haze?"

"It is unlikely," the keeper said. "During the Haze, her primary goal is to mate and breed. The idea of blood in her mouth is highly unappealing."

Drocco exhaled, thinking deeply again. There had to be a way to force her to accept him.

"Does she nest?" the keeper asked, after a long moment.

"For herself."

The keeper frowned. "What do you mean?"

"She has formed a mock nest but it's for her alone, not for both of us."

The keeper crossed his arms, chewing his lip as he thought deeper. "Have you tried to enter it?"

"No," Drocco said, tersely. It annoyed him that he had allowed her the comfort of her pseudo nest and she hadn't even recognized the kindness. "I fear it's the only place she feels safe to sleep, and I need her rested for the typical questioning."

"Typical questioning?"

Drocco nodded. "She takes it well but I know her suffering isn't good for our future connection."

"Suffering?" The head keeper's eyes widened. "She is hurt during the questioning?"

"Of course."

"You cause her pain?"

Drocco shot the man a hard look. "Until she answers my questions, she is hurt repeatedly and continuously. It is the way of the Lox."

The head keeper gasped and paled.

Drocco slowed his pacing, turning to watch the man's reaction. He looked utterly horrified. He swayed on his feet and then clung to the back of the chair before him for support. "What is it?" Drocco asked.

"I thought you were looking to bond with this Omega. I didn't realize she was a prisoner. I apologize for my assumption."

"No, your assumption is correct," Drocco said. "She will be my mate."

The keeper took a deep breath, averting his eyes from Drocco.

"What is it!" Drocco barked.

"It's just... I... I'm not sure..."

"Speak plainly," Drocco ordered. "I have no use for people who cannot speak when needed."

The man got a hold of himself and steadied his stance, dropping his arms to his sides. "Emperor. Your treatment of your Omega may have forever damaged your connection with her."

Drocco growled and clenched his fists, a horrible feeling blooming in his stomach.

The man pressed on. "The Alpha/Omega connection is a delicate one. Although hormones may attract you to one another, there is more that needs to happen for a connection to flourish into the potential for a bond connection."

"Like what?"

"Omegas are certainly submissive and eager to please in their Haze, but they have their own personalities. Our records indicate Omegas have worked in politics, trade, the arts, and the sciences. They are generally intelligent and capable of many feats when their Haze isn't upon them. An Omega needs to feel safe with her Alpha, and once she does, she will tend to try to please him. The most successful relationships I have read about have been where the Omega is completely free of fear. This is highly important. This is what sometimes decides how an Omega chooses her Alpha. They are so vulnerable to everyone that they will be reluctant to let go of an Alpha who makes them feel safe."

Drocco stared at him. "I have not read this anywhere. And you know I have extensive records."

The keeper nodded. "Yes, but I fear you have collected records from Alphas, your Imperial Majesty. Alphas would not record the things that are important to Omegas, only to themselves." His face dropped. "I mean no disrespect, Emperor," he added, quickly. "It's just we have more impartial records, even excerpts from Omega diaries."

Drocco waved away his apology, and he began pacing again in deep thought. Cailyn had always felt fear from him. That was what he had thrived on—it was what he had always thrived on, from everyone. "How do I correct it?" he asked. "How do I get her to feel like I am her Alpha?"

The keeper peered at him. "What is more important to you; your connection with her or finding the other Omegas?"

Drocco stilled again. "Why do I have to choose?"

"Your next steps will be dependent on that decision," the keeper said. "You can continue treating her like a prisoner and you may succeed in getting the information you want, but your connection with her will greatly suffer. I highly doubt you will be able to repair it."

Drocco clenched his teeth. "Or?"

"Or you could work on your connection and make her feel comfortable enough to open up to you."

Drocco stared out of the window as he worked his jaw. He would not be waiting around for her to open up to him, but he needed to ensure their connection was not lost.

"Tell me how to work on our connection."

The keeper nodded, seeming pleased with his answer. "You have to follow your instincts."

"That is what I have been doing," Drocco snapped. "My instincts are to torture those who have lied to me. I do not suffer those that try to deceive me, keeper. It is what has made me Emperor."

"No. Not your instincts as a warrior or Emperor. Your instincts as an Alpha."

Drocco stopped dead, snarling at the keeper. "Are you questioning my competence as an Alpha?"

"No, your Imperial Majesty," the keeper insisted, wincing. "But you haven't ever had to use those instincts in this way before."

"I'm always using my Alpha instincts!" Drocco boomed. "I am a warrior and an Alpha and a leader. I'm all of those things equally!"

The head keeper sucked in a breath and thought for a moment. "When you are in battle and you fight an opponent, you pick up many things about him as you fight?"

"Of course."

"This tells you clues about how to fight him, what his weaknesses are. And you follow those hints and feelings, don't you?"

Drocco nodded.

"This is how you must be with your Omega. Let go of all the things she has done and the pressure of finding the others, and just follow the clues that your body gives you. Your instincts will tell you what she needs."

Drocco thought for a moment. "Will this correct her behavior?"

The head keeper shook his head slowly. "It sounds as though your Omega does not have a submissive personality type, Emperor. If you want that, you will have to find one that does."

"No," Drocco insisted. "It is her. I know she is my destined mate."

"Then her general defiance should be a source of joy for you," the keeper said, his voice quiet. "Not something you want to correct."

"I have found her defiance intriguing in the past but I don't want it directed at me. We should be one; strong and unbreakable."

"But you haven't given her any reason to be on your side, Emperor."

Drocco remained silent as he digested this.

"I suggest you consider if your preference for submissiveness is something you actually desire," the keeper said, "or if it's a stereotypical ideal that has been pushed onto you from past generations. You should not need to change anything about your mate's natural personality to be happy with her."

❖

Drocco stared unseeingly at the research room from the chair he used to sit in to watch Cailyn. He sat there a lot in the past week since he had visited the Records Keep. He hadn't spent any time with Cailyn in his bedroom and had only entered to bring her food in and put it on the table. He hadn't wanted to see the bruises on her neck or deal with her remarks and tears. However, she hadn't been eating. Bowls and plates of food had been left untouched, and he knew he couldn't wait much longer to do something about it.

The head keeper had brought up some interesting points that gave him pause.

Drocco's grandfather had been a formidable Alpha warrior who had revered his Omega and talked about her constantly as he became older and lonely. He said he had the perfect connection with her, and that she was what all Omegas should be—submissive and agreeable. Drocco had taken this to mean that all Omegas were indeed like that, and that any perfect Omega would be such. His father had died long before Drocco had any interest in asking about Omegas, so his grandfather and Torin's grandfather had been the only direct sources he had. But how much of his grandfather's explanations were the ramblings of an old man gone mad from his lost connection to his Omega? How much of Drocco's understanding was tainted by his awe of such a great warrior and powerhouse of an Alpha? He couldn't know.

In truth, much of the research he had collected *had* come from Alphas, some of whom had lost their Omegas. What if they only remembered Haze-affected Omegas because that's what they were pining for? The Omegas had become a myth; beings that relied on the word of man to confirm their existence and nature, and yet the word of man was flawed and unreliable.

His eyes skimmed the room remembering Cailyn's initial rudeness. He had been excited by that and had looked forward to dominating her. She had made him laugh with her displeasure at being called kitten... and he had laughed again at her boldness to lift her juicy pussy to his mouth to get what she wanted. Certainly, her boldness wasn't actually a turnoff. But he needed a woman who would obey him, not argue and retaliate against him at every turn. Regardless if Cailyn was on his side or not, she did not respect him as an Alpha or an emperor. How could she desire him as her Alpha if that basic respect was lacking? It needed to be corrected.

Drocco stood and began to pace. Clearly, the way he had been going about it had not yet worked but he refused to be at the mercy of her feelings. He needed to find another way. Doing what the head keeper suggested wouldn't be difficult—he was an Alpha after all—but he was suspicious of how it might affect him. He had almost become addicted to having his mouth on her clit and if he followed his instincts, would he become weak? He would not be tamed by Omega pussy.

He glanced around at his research. He must be able to figure out a way to correct a wayward Omega using his Alpha impulses without losing himself in the process and without pandering to her emotions. He began to look through his research, reading the information objectively and connecting the ideas between various reports. He discovered Omegas strengthened their Alphas, not weakened them. He should be fine. Within a few hours, he had refreshed his knowledge and developed the stirrings of a plan.

If following his instincts didn't work... A tightness gripped his throat at the alternative. Giving Cailyn to another Alpha to mate with so he could find another Omega was not an option. He had yet to experience her laugh or her smile or her kisses, and he knew deep within him that there wouldn't be another Omega as beautiful, one who would taste so good, look at him like he was incredible, or flick their hips on his rough thrusts like they couldn't get enough. It didn't matter what other Omegas they found, he would always want Cailyn. He had wanted her before he had discovered her true dynamic, and that was with her defiant nature. It made sense now why that was. She was his. And he had to make her see that, even if by force. She had to bond with him—he needed it and she needed it.

A few hours later, Drocco stood outside his bedroom with a platter of fruits from Cillford cut into small pieces and a range of clothing folded over his forearm. He had spoken to Torin and given orders to be followed regarding his investigation and the Empire. He then issued a blanket order that he not be disturbed. He repositioned the guards to either ends of the corridor so the room felt more private—the door had a triple lock mechanism that meant he could both open and lock it from the inside anyway. Food and drink were to arrive via the guards, but they were never to knock.

He steadied himself, discarding thoughts about finding the other Omegas, about his Empire, about Malloron, and about her betrayal. He abandoned all concerns about everything but the Omega beyond the door. He had his plan, and he needed to follow his instincts for it to work. Twisting the handle, he entered the room.

CHAPTER TEN

CAILYN

Cailyn rocked in her cocoon, thoughts rolling ceaselessly through her mind; everything the Mothers had said about Alphas, her training, poor plans of how to get out of her situation, and the fact that she hadn't been lucky enough to die from Drocco's hand.

She was in a worse situation than she had been before. Drocco hadn't killed her, but he would certainly make her suffer like he always did. He may even be more careful about punishing her so that she didn't die. And yet, he was the best option for her death. Yes, she could starve herself—in fact, she welcomed the gnawing emptiness of her stomach— but it wasn't as effective as having the emperor crush her quickly.

She considered how she could aggravate him again. Maybe she could goad him with more lies about other men. She frowned. He had been upset about that. Had he been jealous? She shook the thought from her head. There was no way that he truly wanted her for who she was. Any possessive thought he had was due to his unwillingness to share something that no one else had. As soon as he found the other Omegas, he would discard her. He was fooling himself if he thought he would not be enticed by other Omegas.

Her thoughts revolved in her mind, so consuming and continuously, she barely heard the door open, but when it shut, she stilled. Shuffling and soft sounds reached her, but the door did not open again immediately like it had done since he tried to kill her. He remained in the room. She curled up tighter, hoping he would go to sleep and leave her alone.

"Cailyn."

Cailyn started at the sound of her name. She froze, suddenly unsure what to do.

She listened again, a silence building.

"Cailyn, come here."

Her heart began to pound. He had never called her by her name before—something was wrong. She considered staying in her blankets but she couldn't ignore him. She was mentally and emotionally weak, and her resistance was depleted.

She climbed slowly out of her cocoon and peered over to the other side of the bedroom. Drocco sat on the couch next to the table, his black eyes watching her. He was bare-chested and barefoot but wore black trousers. She dropped her eyes and padded towards him slowly, trying to prepare for whatever pain he was about to issue this time.

She slowed to a stop before him, staring at the floor, as the hint of his scent began to surround her. "Emperor," she began, shakily. "I will not—"

"Drocco."

Cailyn paused, unsure what he meant by his interruption. "Um… Yes, Emperor."

"Drocco," he repeated. "You will call me Drocco."

Cailyn stared at him, confused.

He held out a piece of fabric.

She frowned, glancing at him as she took it. Lifting it up, she shook it out to see a red tunic dress. She looked back at him.

Drocco simply nodded.

Fumbling, she put the dress on, confused by his change of heart about her lack of clothing. Maybe he was trying to unsettle her.

"Come here."

Cailyn stepped forward tentatively until she stood right in front of his legs, wide on the couch.

In a swift move, he lifted her up and maneuvered her onto his lap, her legs straddling his hips. Cailyn kept her eyes averted. She leaned away from him, balancing on his one wide, outstretched hand on her back.

She sat, not looking at him. She didn't care what he was doing—whatever his new plan was, she would find a way to annoy and anger him so he would wish she were dead.

A faint, steady, rumble caught her attention, and as it swelled she realized it came from him. He was purring.

She stared at him, her eyes wide in shock as the strength of his purr increased, the vibrations seemingly penetrating the space between them and seeping into her.

Cailyn closed her eyes and sighed as it became stronger, working into her and cutting through her emotional gloom. She had heard about the Alpha purr at the Omega Compound. It had been touted as one of the few good things about Alphas, and something only they could do for Omegas that no others could do so satisfyingly. Many of the younger Omegas had no idea how that could be, but it was talked about fondly and some of the older Omegas from her childhood had been reduced to tears after discussing it.

Cailyn could see why. It was incredible. The vibrations pierced deep into her, bringing with it a soothing unlike anything she had felt before. All of her emotional turmoil and distress stirred and bubbled through her, rising up only to dissipate into nothing, leaving an immense feeling of complete relief beaming through her. It overwhelmed her so thoroughly, she burst into tears. She cried for her lost freedom, for the secrets she'd revealed, and for her lost family of Omegas, but the solid weight of her depression lifted.

As her tears petered out, she realized his hand on her back was drawing her closer to him. She opened her eyes to see Drocco still staring at her, though she couldn't read the expression on his face. He drew her closer and closer until she lay on his chest, his rumbling purr vibrating through her cheek. She kept still, wondering what the point of this was. Indeed she felt better, in fact, she felt almost content, but that was his purr, not him. He was still a monstrous savage. She lay on him, waiting for what he was going to do next, but nothing happened. As she continued to listen to his purr, she realized it had a husky quality, similar to the husk in his laugh. She pressed her cheek into him further, trying to get as much of the vibration as she could and sighed again, enjoying the comfort of it. Before she knew it she was relaxing into him, drowsy with peaceful sleep.

Cailyn had no idea how long they sat there but she found herself waking up still straddling the emperor. She had every intention of getting off him, but he still purred, and she found she couldn't, and didn't want to, move away from that.

He seemed to sense her restlessness. He lifted her again, and she made a pitiful noise at being moved away from the source of her comfort, but he simply fixed her sideways on his lap and returned her to his chest.

She lay for a few long moments and then a sweet, familiar smell filled her nose. When she opened her eyes, Drocco held a piece of fruit to her lips. She opened her mouth and he placed it inside. It was something she'd had before. She couldn't place where she'd had it or its name, but it was tasty. It pulled on memories she couldn't quite reach, memories swathed in darkness. He fed her another piece, and she savored it, the juicy, sweetness sparking her appetite.

He fed her a range of fruit from a platter on the table, some of them she loved, others she disliked. He didn't bring any she refused to her lips again. Finally, her hunger was sated, and she fell asleep again against his vibrating chest.

Cailyn lost all track of time. The days blurred together, she didn't know how much time had passed and couldn't even guess. The only thing she cared about was that purr. Drocco kept her against his chest all the time and stayed with her constantly. He bathed with her, lathered and rinsed her, he sat with her while she ate, sometimes feeding her, and he kept her pressed against his chest to sleep on him as he sat on the couch. She had no idea when he slept or when he ate. She wasn't sure she cared about that. His purr kept her in a state of contentment that she didn't want to come out of. If she could stay in that oblivious state, then the reality of her situation didn't matter.

She convinced herself of this even further because Drocco didn't speak. He didn't say a word to her. And she had no reason to say anything to him. They simply existed.

However, she couldn't ignore the normal physical reaction she always had for him. She remained in a constant state of arousal, and it became stronger every day it wasn't addressed. She could feel his arousal too when she sat on his lap. And yet he never moved to touch her or to relieve himself.

As her body's other major concerns, such her hunger and her distress, were tended to, her need to mate with him increased. She ignored it, choosing to lose herself in his purr, but after a while, it became almost unbearable.

At one point, she sat on his lap, her face buried into his neck, breathing him in, and she began to rub herself on the hardness underneath her without even realizing it at first. Drocco growled and instantly her slick streamed from her.

Lifting her up, he carried her to the bed and placed her down. She sat upright, watching him warily as he undressed, his eyes remaining on her.

A trembling of fear fluttered through her. Regardless of the pleasurable nature of their mating, it had always ended in unbearable pain. Perhaps her respite was over. She sucked a breath in as he lay down beside her, ready for what may come.

She waited, but nothing happened. Turning to glance at him, she saw he lay naked on the bed, his massive and muscled body stretched along almost the entire length. Her eyes were drawn to his cock, hard and upright.

She glanced back up to his eyes, desire and demand stared back at her. He wanted her. He expected her to mate with him—to follow her instincts and relieve them both. But she couldn't. Not only had she never initiated sex before, she had not chosen him. They were not a couple, and just because he purred for her, it did not mean she wanted him as a bonded mate. He would have to accept that.

"Drocco," she began.

His cock twitched and the tip began to ooze.

Cailyn watched transfixed. "Drocco," she whispered.

His cock jumped again, trickling more fluid for her. His potent scent deepened to an intricate aroma that burst around her and seeped into her. Everything she was about to say was lost to her.

Leaning forward, she brought her nose closer to his heavenly scent. Closer and closer still, until she reached his cock. She licked the length of it. He moaned, and the sound spurred her on. Closing her mouth on his tip, she sucked and a rush of desire shuddered through her. Lifting his cock, she sucked and licked him, guided by her instincts to explore every inch of him.

She became aware of his large hand cupping and squeezing her ass and she moved to her knees as his fingers dipped underneath to stroke her.

He breathed heavily, releasing guttural groans as she moved faster with fervor. And the sound of him at her mercy was almost as satisfying as his purr.

She gyrated her hips as his fingers played with her clit, trying to get more pressure, but he seemed to purposely avoid penetrating her. Eventually, she released his cock and glared at him.

He still stared at her—that look of expectation in his eyes. He pressed his fingers against her opening and she whined and widened her knees, trying to sink onto his fingers, but he pulled away.

She snapped her head back to him, a snarl on her lips.

Drocco's expression didn't change. "If you want it, take it." His gravelly, deep, voice instantly made her wetter.

She looked at his cock, glistening and wet. She had made it like that. Suddenly a heat rose to her face and she lowered her eyes. "I can't," she whispered.

"You can. And you will, Cailyn."

Drocco's hand inched up her dress, slowly and deliberately. His hand was rough against her skin and she moaned as it scraped up her back, sending a scatter of tingles all over her. He slowly pulled her dress over her head, and began playing with her already hard nipples, dragging his nails across her body and dipping his fingertips lower to brush her clit.

She gasped and moaned and hummed at the sensations building in her. Everything he did enhanced her pleasure, but her neglected pussy made her frustrated. She squirmed, uncomfortable with the amount of slick she was producing, and looked again at his cock. She wanted it.

Drocco suddenly lifted her up and lowered her onto him, her legs either side of him. As her wet core pressed onto him, she rubbed against him, slathering his hardness with her slick. She moaned as his shaft and tip pressed against her clit and leaned forward to place her hands on the bed, either side of his torso.

He lay looking at her with that same expression, and for a moment, an annoyance coursed through her that he wasn't touching her. His hands were on the fucking bed instead of on her—caressing her, petting her, moving her to where he wanted. Then his cock twitched underneath her.

She looked down between them. Reaching down, she lined up his cock to her entrance and sunk down on it. She groaned, as did Drocco, as she lowered all the way down onto him. She stilled, gasping at the incredible feeling of being filled and stretched and then began to rock on him.

She remained leaning over, her weight on her hands, watching their joining as her pleasure built. His thick cock shone with her slick, and as she rode him faster, lifting herself all the way to his tip and back down, a wild sense of perverse pleasure rocked through her. Fuck, it was so good!

The harder she rode, the more powerful the sensations and soon she cried out in utter ecstasy, her fists bunching the sheets.

"Look at me." Drocco's voice was quiet but demanding.

She lifted her head. His eyes were half-lidded and he breathed heavily. Her desire spiked, sending a clench to her core.

"Beautiful," he breathed.

He lifted his head up toward her, his stomach muscles bunching up to rub her hard nipples. He grabbed her ass cheek and began to yank her hips down on him, guiding her faster and faster until her head rolled back and she almost screamed.

"Look at me, Cailyn."

She forced herself to look back at him. His face had moved closer and his eyes drank in every inch of her face. His other hand scooped up her hair in a tight grip and, as he slammed her hips down on him, almost violently, he brought his lips to hers with the softest brush of a kiss.

She came hard, the explosion of intense bliss causing her entire body to twist and shudder. He kept her steady and swallowed all of her screams and moans as he deepened the kiss. She kissed him back, reveling in the roughness of his tongue, his breath in her mouth, and the claiming nature of his grip. Was there any part of this man that didn't taste good? He slammed his knot in, grunting and moaning in her mouth as he came, but wouldn't release her from his kiss. He spread his hand on her ass, keeping them pressed together.

Cailyn tried to pull away, fear returning ten-fold as she realized he had knotted her, and what that meant, but he gripped her hair harder, slowing his kiss to suck on her tongue and nibble on her lower lip. She remained tense, waiting for the questioning to start, but he seemed content to simply kiss her.

As he continued to explore her mouth, she relaxed slightly, noticing how securely they were locked together. It felt... strange—as though she was claiming his cock. As he kissed her longer, his purr returned and she relaxed further, kissing him back.

The intimacy of his lips on hers affected her in a way she hadn't been prepared for. Not only was she learning a new taste and feel of him, but his approach surprised her. Drocco was kissing her tenderly; still claiming, still intense, but also careful and lingering, as though he relished her.

Eventually, he slowly pulled away to look at her. "How many men?"

Cailyn stared into his ink-like eyes, breathless from his kisses and drowsy from their mating. "Just you."

His eyes ran over her face. "Just me?"

"Just you, Drocco."

His purr deepened and he lay back on the bed. She waited for him to smirk or laugh or question why she lied, but he simply watched her.

She lay on his chest, sighing as his purr rumbled against her, coaxing her to sleep.

When she next stirred, she lay on her side on the bed, her leg over Drocco's hip while his hand still held her ass. His purr still vibrated from him but he seemed asleep. She stared at him for a moment. Even in his sleep, he looked rugged and wild. Sighing, she rolled away from him and headed to the washroom. As she used the toilet and washed, she realized that she and Drocco had fully mated, with a knot that had remained inside her until it shrunk. That meant he could get her pregnant. She pondered the possibility before dismissing it. Normally an Omega's chances of pregnancy increased in her Haze and it was still possible through normal mating, especially when a high attraction existed between the couple. However, with Cailyn's blocks messing up her Haze cycle, she suspected it would be difficult for her to get pregnant when not in her Haze.

She couldn't deny that she was attracted to Drocco. Regardless of the fact that she was his prisoner, he was the kind of Alpha many Omegas would want as a bonded mate. In fact, many of the younger Omegas had been arguing the logic of staying hidden when Omegas were trained in the Talent. Some of them had petitioned the Mothers for a change in the rules to allow Talent-crafter Omegas to leave the compound to find an Alpha or Beta mate to create a life with. Of course, many of them hadn't even been through the required training to leave the compound—they seemed to have high-flown ideas about what the Eastern Land cities and territories were like, and even though some admitted being scared to leave, they had plenty of ideas of what the future could hold for Omegas.

She headed back to the room, back to Drocco, but paused at the edge of the bed. She turned to glance at her own bed, in the corner on the floor. She hadn't slept there in what felt like weeks, and yet that was where she had been most comfortable. Did she really want to return to the bed with the emperor? The place where she had suffered, and with the man who had made her suffer?

She turned and headed toward her bed and slowed to a stop halfway there as the potency of his purr began to fade. She turned toward him, indecision clouding her. She wanted to be close to his purr but not on the bed. She stood watching him and suddenly noticed he was awake, watching her back.

"Would you like me to join you, Cailyn?" he asked. Once again his voice sent a shiver through her.

"Yes," she whispered.

He got up from the bed, unfolding to his full height. Cailyn's eyes widened as she took him in. She had forgotten how big he was. She shrunk back as he strode toward her, wondering how the hell he was going to fit in her little makeshift bed. This was a bad idea.

He scooped her up and carried her the rest of the way to her bed, then carefully knelt to allow her to lift the pile of duvets and sheets.

It took some shifting and shuffling and readjustment before they were both encased, head to toe, by all the duvets, blankets and cushions, and a nervousness clawed at Cailyn as she wondered if she was doing the right thing. She had allowed him into her private space. The space where she felt safe. Why destroy that? But as soon as Drocco drew her into his arms, and her head lay on his rumbling chest, all other thoughts disappeared. His scent expanded into the small enclosed area and she sighed at the comfort of it.

Drocco lowered his head, his mouth against her forehead. "I'm pleased you allowed me into your nest."

Cailyn's drowsiness fled and she was suddenly awake. Her nest? Her mind raced, trying to remember what she had been told about nesting Omegas. The Mothers had spoken about it, but it was so early in her training, she couldn't remember. It felt like it was important. Disturbed, she found she couldn't relax, even with that thick, heavy rumble coming from the broad chest against her.

She fidgeted and turned, worried thoughts rolling through her mind. Finally, Drocco pulled her higher to kiss her thoroughly before taking a nipple into his mouth, erasing all worries from her mind.

Life became a simple series of meeting her base needs. When she was hungry, Drocco made sure she ate. When she was tired, Drocco's purr rocked her to sleep. When she was restless, plagued by thoughts she couldn't control, he shifted his weight on top of her, pinning her to the nest and making her feel secure and protected. When she had even a spark of arousal, Drocco's mouth was on her body, building her to that incredible high, which meant he fucked her all the time.

Gone was the Drocco who demanded with a single look—he took her roughly and completely, owning her body and claiming it with every spearing thrust of his cock, every flick of his tongue, every deep, breathtaking kiss. She hated that she loved it. She hated that she rode his face so enthusiastically— that it was so pleasurable to lick and suck every part of him. And when in her right mind, she was embarrassed that she reveled in the vulgar pleasure that came from putting herself on display, widening her legs to spread her slick-drenched pussy so eagerly to entice him to slam into her—all without him needing to even utter a word.

Every touch brought her so much complex bliss she'd never experienced before, she couldn't get enough. The fear of his knot had been replaced by a strange satisfaction whenever she locked her muscles onto that intimate part of him. Her pussy seemed to think his cock belonged to it, and an odd thrill began to build every time it happened.

Once, while on all fours and locked on to him behind her, Drocco grabbed her arms and lifted her back toward him, pinning her elbows together with one hand. He kissed and licked the back of her neck and reached round to squeeze and slap her breasts, wringing her nipples and clawing his nails over her stomach. That was all it took for her to come again, shuddering on his knot and clenching onto every inch of him buried inside her. He cursed in exclamation, pulling her into his arms and telling her how amazing she was. He made her orgasm multiple times on his knot. It meant that their mating seemed to last for ages, and she was always exhausted after.

It was a good thing really. She tried not to allow herself to think of anything beyond the room or beyond her senses. What was the point? She couldn't escape if her Talent didn't work. She was at his mercy and, at the moment, he was being attentive. She allowed herself to drown in the overwhelming sensations.

She became familiar with the subtle differences in his purr. When he slept it was lighter than normal, when he was distracted it was erratic, and when he was satisfied it was luxuriously heavy. The amazing thing was, she began to feel safe and comfortable. It was even pleasurable when he tucked her into his chest to sleep, running his hands all over her, petting her and gently squeezing parts of her body.

However, as time passed, she began to wonder about his motives. Drocco was an intelligent Alpha, capable of planning and executing sophisticated missions to conquer the Eastern Lands. She noticed he would always collect their food and drink from the locked door when she was indisposed; sleeping, drowsy from sex or using the washroom. He was smart enough to try to keep her attention away from those occurrences. So what was his plan with her? Every so often, the thought niggled her that maybe once he had his fill, he would pass her on to another Alpha. Or he would move on to another female. The idea lowered her mood and sparked both jealousy and anger before she caught it and scolded herself. They were not a couple, she had to remember that. Whatever came next, after he tired of her, she had to prepare for it.

She began to climb out of the nest more to spend time sitting at the wall-wide window, behind the curtain. The city beyond the forest had changed from the time she first looked out at it. Broken buildings had been knocked down or mended, the general cream coloring of the buildings had been decorated with patterns of red or black, marking it as Lox Empire. Cailyn stared out at it, wondering how long she had actually been in the room.

One day, Drocco lifted the curtain and sat next to her with a small plate, watching the city as he passed her fruit. They had remained in silence for most of the time since he had tried to strangle her, and she hadn't forced any kind of conversation for fear of breaking the contentment she so desperately needed at the time. But now that there were questions on her tongue, she didn't know how to phrase what she wanted to say.

"You have been very thoughtful lately," Drocco said, his eyes on the city.

Cailyn glanced at him. "How long have I been here?" she asked tentatively, taking an orange segment.

"Does it matter?"

Cailyn shrugged. Maybe it didn't. "I'm wondering what your plans are for me."

Drocco held out an apple chunk. "It's not important. I'm looking after you, that's all you need to know."

Cailyn took the fruit. "Looking after me by keeping me captive?"

Drocco turned to look at her. "Is there anything you are lacking?"

"My freedom."

Drocco placed the plate down next to him and pulled her onto his lap, keeping her facing the city. "You think you want that, but you don't."

Cailyn tensed. "You can't tell me what I want."

Drocco's hand slipped between her thighs. "I can."

Cailyn huffed, squeezing her thighs together but failing to trap his hand as his fingers climbed higher.

"You are easier to read than you think," he murmured into her ear, his fingers brushing gently against her pussy. "I can detect your moods, I can tell what you need and when you need it. I know what you like... what you dislike... your preferences."

"I preferred it when you were silent," she snapped. "As soon as you open your mouth, you spoil things."

He grabbed her hair and yanked her head back, lowering to press his nose against her neck. "I know you don't want it to be true, but that is the benefit of being in close proximity to your Alpha."

"Just because you can tell when my body is aroused doesn't mean you know what I want," Cailyn replied, evenly. "And it doesn't mean you're my Alpha."

His mouth moved up her neck. "Did you know you purr in your sleep?"

Cailyn jolted in surprise. She twisted in his grip to look at him. "W-what?"

Drocco relaxed his hold on her, staring back into her eyes, a slight smirk on his face. "You would not purr if you wanted to leave. You would not purr for an Alpha that isn't yours. You would not nest with me if you weren't preparing for a life with me, Cailyn. You are content here."

Cailyn stared at him in shock. Omegas at the compound never purred. It was something they only did with or for their chosen Alphas. "No," she whispered.

A flash of irritation crossed Drocco's face. He lifted his head to look at the city, but his jaw was hard. "No what, Cailyn?"

Cailyn swallowed. She turned back to look at the city too, her thoughts racing. She remembered now. Generally, nesting Omegas were preparing a place for their pregnancy, but it could also be a place they created to simply feel safe. Yes. That's what she had done. He had tortured her after all. As for her purring... "I don't know if that's true, Drocco."

"You don't have to know." His fingers played with her lazily and she tried not to be distracted by her body's response. "You just have to listen to your body. When you do, you will feel the instinct to purr. Just like I felt when to do it for you."

Cailyn was speechless. There it was. She was being primed into letting her body's natural instincts take over her natural thoughts, something he knew she didn't want, and she had been allowing it to happen, distracted by the comfort of his purr and the pleasure he wrecked on her. A small part of her wondered if it really was a terrible thing. She had been content over these past... however long it was, hadn't she?

No. It hadn't been real. She had been distressed to the point of suicide and had suffered through his attempt to murder her. His purr would, of course, force her to cling to him and he had manipulated her with that knowledge. Furthermore, he was an emperor. How could he be spending day after day with her without needing to leave and tend to his

Empire? He had a plan to bring her to heel. He was manipulating her—even now, with his hand between her legs as he discussed this.

"Cailyn," he murmured, kissing her ear as his fingers zeroed in on her clit. "I know you don't like being called kitten, but you should know, your purr is very... cute."

Cailyn gritted her teeth against the tingling sensations building in her. "It's not real."

Drocco's fingers froze. "What?"

"It's not real. You are the first and only man I've been with—the only Alpha. My Omega impulses are all over the place. They can't be trusted."

Drocco was silent for a long while. "You don't want to trust them," he growled accusingly. "You have never wanted to trust them."

"I'm just trying to point out that you cannot keep assuming you are my Alpha. You are most likely mistaken."

Drocco's whole body tensed. "You still deny it?"

"Yes."

Drocco pushed Cailyn off of his lap and stood abruptly. She watched him stalk to the other side of the bedroom and pull clothes out of the closet to dress.

"Where are you going?" she asked, alarmed. If he was getting dressed, that meant he was leaving.

"I'm tired of all this denial," he hollered, yanking on his shirt. "I'm going to find a Beta female to fuck. One who will submit willingly and beg me to bond with her."

Cailyn narrowed her eyes and slowly got up, a sudden heat flaring all over her body. "If you leave, you will not come back in my nest."

"I will fuck you whenever I want," Drocco shot back. "And you will want me because that's how your body always responds, even though it supposedly can't be trusted." He pulled on his boots. "If you don't want to claim me, you will not mind sharing."

Cailyn trembled with a rage so intense, her mind had only one focus. She stepped toward him, slowly crossing the room, her fists clenched. "If you fuck another female, I will *kill* you."

Drocco stilled, his gaze intensifying as he took her in. His nostrils flared and something changed in his eyes. He turned and strode to the door.

Cailyn ran toward him, determined to rip his fucking face off, but the door slammed behind him before she got there. A hot, white fury seared through her and she shrieked a string of curses as she pounded the door with all her might. Then she turned on the room and destroyed everything she could reach, screaming and yelling obscenities in her anguish.

By the time she calmed, the room was an absolute wreck. Water and food were splattered everywhere, the bed was a mess, the table and chairs were overturned and even part of the curtain limped from its rail.

Cailyn sat in the middle of the room, tormented by the idea of Drocco with another woman. She sobbed and rocked, trying to reason with herself that it didn't matter, but it did. He would come back to her smothered with another woman's scent, and she would still open her legs for him. He knew it. And she couldn't deny that her extreme reaction aligned with his theories. She had become emotionally attached to him somehow. She wanted him for herself, everything about him. Not just his tongue, his cock, his husky purr, or those liquid jet-black eyes, she also wanted his laugh, his dominance, his thundering demands… she wanted *him.* The monster she had always despised—that she still despised. When had it come to this?

She crawled to the strewn blankets of her nest and found the one most saturated with his scent before curling up on it, her tears still spilling down her cheeks.

CHAPTER ELEVEN

DROCCO

Drocco stood on the other side of his bedroom door listening to his Omega's jealous rage. It was the most erotic thing he'd ever heard, and he desperately wanted to storm back in and fuck her senseless.

He knew for certain now that he did not want a submissive Omega. When Cailyn had threatened him, her voice low and possessive, her eyes flashing, her body ready to pounce, he almost came in his pants. She was tiny and yet had outright threatened him if he lay with another. A submissive woman wouldn't have dared; they might have cried, or become emotionally distressed, but none would have threatened him like a warrior, as Cailyn had, nor charged at him like they could actually do damage. It turned him on more than anything she had done so far—and that was a feat in itself since her every action, and every sound, made him hard.

As she quietened, he forced himself to move away from the door and head to Torin's office. His plan was working, and now he had to be careful not to spoil it with his own eagerness.

He navigated down the corridor, feeling slightly strange to suddenly be out of the four walls he had been in for so long. His time spent in the room with Cailyn had been more satisfying than anything he had ever experienced. He hadn't missed anything outside of the bedroom; she gave him everything he needed. He could understand everything his grandfather had said, and even what the head keeper had told him. Cailyn drew out every part of him that made him an Alpha—parts of him he had never accessed before. There were things he instinctively knew and did for her that he had never done before, like purr. He hadn't cared, tried, or known how to even attempt to do it before, but Cailyn's distress and subsequent desire for it had made it a natural occurrence.

Their sexual connection had been restored and had flourished. When she gave in to her desires, she teased and enticed him deliciously, yet submitted to him more wonderfully than he could have hoped. She touched him more, melted into his kiss, and urged him on when he was rough. She loved having him in her mouth, and her eagerness made her inexperience inconsequential. She came hardest when he pinned her down securely, against the bed, the floor, the table, the wall—any surface—and took her like a fucking animal. He had never been able to be so wild, so free, with any other. It both settled and strengthened him in a way he couldn't even begin to comprehend.

She was made for him, which he already knew. She hadn't smiled for him properly yet, but that would come. Soon she would have to admit her emotional attachment to him and declare him hers. Her sleepy, sexy, trill of a purr proved it. However, even if she still continued to deny it, it didn't matter. He could tell her Haze was close. He had scented the sweet hint of it in her anger before he left. Hopefully, if he left her seething, she would be primed to go into her Haze not long after he returned. In her Haze, she would tell him everything he wanted to know and he would be able to breed her. The Haze was the perfect solution to everything and was what he had been waiting for.

When he arrived at Torin's office, a servant redirected him to the main meeting room.

"Drocco," Torin said surprised, as Drocco entered. "This is a pleasant surprise." Torin stood by the back wall with a couple of Talent-crafters. He had grown a light dusting of stubble on his face, making him look older and somewhat fiercer.

"How long has it been?" Drocco asked, sitting at the large table in the middle of the room.

"Nearly three months," Torin said. He sniffed and then smirked. "It seems like things are going well."

Drocco grinned. "Indeed. Anything I should know?"

Torin sobered. "Malloron."

Drocco clenched his jaw. "What about him?"

"He has been persistent—sending letters and insisting meetings with you."

"What happened to his threat to withdraw his offer?"

183

"I don't know. Every time we speak he refuses to discuss anything unless you are present."

Drocco took note of Torin's position in the room and the Talent-crafters against the back wall. "You're meeting with him now?"

Torin nodded. In a few moments."

"You are still allowing portals to come into the palace?" Drocco asked, harshly.

"Lox crafters are controlling it, Drocco," Torin insisted. "They are the ones creating the portal now. Malloron has no control."

Drocco glanced at the Talent-crafters. Torin had always been the cautious and careful one—it was doubtful he would do something that would put them in danger.

Drocco stood up. "I will speak with him."

Torin hesitated. "I don't think that is wise."

"I am the emperor, and it is me he has requested. I'll find out what he wants."

"You have just come from your Omega's nest, Drocco," Torin pointed out. "I don't think it's wise for you to speak to him immediately after seeing her. He isn't that important."

Drocco narrowed his eyes. "How many times do I need to repeat myself with you, Torin?"

Torin sighed and looked him over. "All right. Just remember that he is likely to be frustrated that you have not been available for the last few meetings."

Drocco nodded. "Understood."

"We're ready, Commander," the nearest Talent-crafter called.

Torin told Drocco where to stand and how to signal to the Talent-crafters when he wanted to end the meeting.

"Ready?" Torin asked.

Drocco nodded.

The Talent-crafters closed their eyes, their hands clasped, and a thin sheet of glistening magic appeared in the air before him and slowly morphed, many brilliant colors jumping within it until the center cleared to reveal Malloron in his rich clothing.

Malloron's eyes widened in surprise. It seemed he hadn't expected to see Drocco either.

"Greetings, King Malloron," Drocco began. "May Eiros thrive and be weal—"

"Is it true you have an Omega?" Malloron demanded, leaning forward.

Drocco nodded. "Yes."

Malloron stared him for a moment, his dark eyes wild, before leaning back in his chair and composing himself. "Congratulations, Emperor. I take back all insinuations I made that you would not be able to do it."

Drocco simply dipped his head. "I appreciate it. Is that the only reason for the urgency for us to talk? I assume you realize by now that I will not be agreeing to your terms."

Malloron lifted his head in a slow nod. "Yes, I realize." He was silent for a moment. "I believe I can offer something else."

"Like what?"

"Your Omega's obedience."

Drocco tensed, a snarl forming on his face. "Speak again, King Malloron. And I advise you to be careful which words you choose to repeat."

"It's no secret that you have had trouble with your Omega, Emperor," Malloron said, shrugging. "I can help you."

Drocco could barely contain his anger. Malloron couldn't know unless someone from inside the palace had been watching Drocco and sending Malloron updates. There were still spies within Lox Palace. He glared at Malloron, wishing the man was really in front of him. He would love to drive his axe through the man's brain and be rid of him.

"It's no secret, Emperor," Malloron repeated, a gleam in his dark eyes. "You don't need to look at me so murderously. The entire Eastern Lands is discussing it. They say you have stormed out of your room numerous times, left her alone for days, and failed to breed her in her Haze. I'm sure they have most of the details wrong, but whatever the reason is that you have not breeded her yet, I can help you."

"I will not discuss my Omega with you," Drocco growled. "If you dare bring her up again—"

"You cannot be selfish," Malloron said, his voice harsh. "Your Omega represents much for all of us. Your warriors might be too afraid to say it, but I'm not. It has been four or five months since you've had her. You have neither breeded her nor discovered where the other Omegas are. Those two things are your only responsibilities, and you are failing them."

Drocco roared, a vicious rage charging through him as he stepped closer to the portal. Torin tried to call his attention, but he barely saw the movement in the corner of his eye. "You have no right to comment on my Omega or my responsibilities, you *fuck*! You're not even within my Empire. I owe you *nothing*. The only Alphas that can demand anything from me are my warriors and you are not among them! You are never to request another meet—"

"I apologize," Malloron said, holding up his palms. "I apologize, Emperor. Please forgive me."

Drocco breathed heavy, his fingers itching for his axe, but his anger quickly quietened when he noticed that Malloron remained calm and collected. A horrible feeling came over him as he stared at the other Alpha.

Malloron had been trying to goad him into saying something revealing. Clearly, he hadn't gotten what he wanted otherwise he wouldn't have apologized so quickly, but Drocco's reaction must have told him something. Drocco glanced at Torin, whose expression was grim.

"I have a proposition for you, Emperor Drocco," Malloron said, quickly. "Hear me out and then I'll never contact you or request anything from you again." He continued speaking, not giving Drocco the chance to respond. "I will give you, or your Talent-crafters, the ability to get your Omega to reveal the location of the other Omegas, in a painless, easy way. She won't even remember having told you."

Drocco narrowed his eyes. "This is through use of the Talent?"

"Yes," Malloron said. "It's a subtle and delicately crafted spell that will get her to tell you all she knows."

"Why do you assume she hasn't already told me?"

Malloron lifted his shoulders, a faint smile on his lips. "She very well could have, but can you trust that she speaks the truth? No one knows what happened to the Omegas and you have only found one. Her discovery could be the result of a myriad of different things. Wouldn't you want to know?"

"There are ways of discovering things without using the Talent, Malloron," Drocco replied. "I have no desire to tie myself to you simply to discover if she has told me the truth."

Malloron tilted his head, his eyes narrowing. "You have soul-bonded her," he said slowly. "That is how you know."

"You can play your guessing games on your own time," Drocco said, annoyed.

"All right," Malloron said, with an air of defeat. "All right. You drive a hard bargain."

"I do not want—"

"I'll give you the complete history of your Omega," Malloron said. "From birth to the moment you met her."

Drocco's eyes narrowed. "What do you mean?"

"I will give you a spell that will show you everything about her," Malloron said, quietly. "Even things she doesn't know herself. It's a complex spell—I will need a day to weave it."

Drocco eyed him. Every part of Cailyn's history in his hands... "What do you want for it?"

"The same as I asked for before—your process and methods to creating an army and two of your troops."

Drocco stared at him as he thought. Cailyn's accurate history laid out for him without him having to force her to tell him anything. It would certainly take the pressure off their relationship while still aiding the Lox. Although it was dependent on the Talent, it was sorely tempting. "Let us have another meeting tomorrow, and I'll give you an answer then. Have it ready just in case."

Malloron scowled. "So you will make me create this spell and not tell me if you're going to accept it?"

"Yes," Drocco said, simply. "Tomorrow. Same time." He signaled to the Talent-crafters, and the portal melted into nothing.

"Get out," Torin ordered the Talent-crafters before turning to Drocco, his face sour.

A harsh annoyance rose in Drocco. If Torin was angry, something was wrong that Drocco hadn't yet seen.

"Why did you let that happen?" Torin scolded. "You told me never to discuss your Omega with anyone, and then you go and discuss her with *Malloron!*"

"I tried not to," Drocco scowled, dropping into a chair. "He antagonized me."

"Of course he is going to antagonize you! You have an Omega!"

"What did I reveal?"

Torin frowned. "You can't see it?"

"No," Drocco snapped. "I didn't reveal anything by what I said."

Torin shook his head, disbelievingly. "He will know now by how angry you became, and by the fact you're even thinking about his proposal, that you care about this Omega."

"He already thinks I soul-bonded her. He already knew that I want that."

"No. He was guessing," Torin pointed out. "Just like he was guessing that you might not be happy with the progress you are making with her. And if he had any suspicions that you were simply taking advantage of her dynamic, they are gone. He knows you want her for yourself, permanently."

Drocco digested this. "It means nothing. What can he do? His spies won't be able to get to her." Cailyn was in his own bedroom, in a tightly secure part of the palace and guarded in multiple circumferences by warriors he had trained almost from birth. Additionally, the whole floor had been protected by Talent-disabling charms. The chances of anyone getting to her was minute.

"I suppose that is true," Torin said, thoughtfully. "But I'm concerned about what he seemed to pretend to know."

"What do you mean?"

"He knows no more than anyone in the palace or even anyone in Ashens, and yet he made some connections that seemed accurate."

Drocco growled at him. "I told you months ago that I didn't want any more of his fucking spies in this palace."

"And I just told you he doesn't have any more information than any Lox warrior or citizen of Ashens," Torin shot back. "You were only visibly angry in front of your staff once. He guessed you haven't breeded her, and he assumed that you had access to her during her Haze. He isn't getting it from spies, he is simply smart. And you cannot afford to engage in conversation with him again until you are free of all influences, including your Omega!"

Drocco shot from his chair, advancing toward Torin. "Who the fuck do you think you're speaking to? What gives you the right to speak to me that way, Torin? To give me orders about my mate?" He pushed his chest into Torin's, growling at the nerve of the man.

"Our history," Torin glowered. "You told me when we were seventeen that if you ever found your Omega, to remind you that you were a warrior too."

Drocco froze. That was when his grandfather had died; shriveled and weak and crying for his Omega— nothing like the man he had looked up to since birth.

"So now I'm telling you," Torin continued. "You are a leader, you run an Empire. I'm not saying you're weak, Drocco, but you must remember that your hormones will be turbulent until you soul-bond."

Drocco's anger drained away. He moved away from Torin and lowered into his chair.

"The feelings are a natural aspect of being an Alpha, but I don't think you should concern yourself with Empire business until you soul-bond," Torin said.

Drocco snapped a look at him. "Understand that I trust and respect you, Torin, but I will not remove myself from my Empire just because I am an Alpha."

"Even if it will be used against you?" Torin said.

"Yes," Drocco said. "That is why *you* are my Commander and not an Alpha. You will keep me grounded like you always do. Let's move on from this discussion."

Torin exhaled harshly, moving to sit next to Drocco. "Are you seriously considering Malloron's offer?"

"Yes."

"Why?"

"I want to know my Omega."

"You don't believe what she tells you?" Torin asked, scratching his stubbled cheek.

Drocco thought carefully before he responded. "I do. But I don't know if she has been brainwashed or tricked. She comes across as very knowledgeable, but there is something lacking in her knowledge of her own background and family. If the Talent is involved, I wouldn't be surprised if it has been used on her adversely. If I am to soul-bond her, I think I should know everything about her—even the things she doesn't know about herself."

Torin stared at Drocco for a moment and then relaxed into a wary smile. "That is the smartest thing I have heard you say since she arrived."

"But I don't trust Malloron at all," Drocco said.

Torin nodded. "No. I could speak to our Talent-crafters to see if they are able to create such a spell, but it seems it would be involved, complex, and require immense skill."

They were both silent for a moment, in thought.

"Is there any way to assess if what he gives us is harmful?" Drocco asked.

Torin nodded. "Yes, our Talent-crafters can assess it. But I doubt he will harm your Omega. Reports suggest he has always been desperate to find the Omegas. It's likely he wants to know what you know."

"It could be harmful to me, then."

Torin shot him a disbelieving look. "It's highly doubtful. He will know he is no match for the Lox army, who will all want to avenge you until their dying breath—even more so now that you have actually found an Omega. Also, there are Lox in the Western Lands now. We have warriors in his territory."

Drocco raised his eyebrows. He had ordered a troop to be sent to the Western Lands before he locked himself in with Cailyn. "They arrived safely and without detection?"

"Yes. If he tries to threaten us, they are in place to deal with him."

Drocco nodded. It was always going to be a risk to deal with Malloron, but he had to weigh up the importance of what he was offering. Was it worth the risk? He considered Cailyn. She was worth it. "So we take his offer."

Torin nodded slowly. "You will give him what he wants?"

"Yes, except actual warriors. It just means we will have to change our methodology."

Torin stood. "All right. I shall see you tomorrow? I can send someone to your bedroom when the meeting time is approaching."

"No," Drocco said, standing with him. "My Omega needs space from me tonight. Fill me in on all that's happened since I have been with her."

The next day, Drocco paced in the meeting room while the Talent-crafters prepared the portal. He had spent the night in his office, away from Cailyn, and after spending so long buried inside her, surrounded by her scent and being able to taste her whenever he wanted, it had been difficult being separated. A foul mood gripped him, and he wanted the meeting over with so he could return to her.

Torin watched him closely, having made clear his annoyance that Drocco had put himself in a situation where his emotions were, yet again, unstable. "Why didn't you summon a Beta female to spend the night with you?"

Drocco looked at Torin, turning to face him before answering. "There are many things we have shared and understood between us during our friendship, Torin. But I cannot make you understand how much more superior my Omega is to me than a Beta female. It cannot compare. She is exquisite. I would rather have nothing than a poor imitation."

Torin's face slackened in shock and for a moment he seemed speechless. He studied Drocco. "We don't have to do this today."

Drocco shot him a look that needed no further elaboration.

Finally, the crafters were ready. They all took their places, one of the crafters standing next to the portal to check whatever Malloron planned to give Drocco.

"Greetings Malloron," Drocco began, when the man appeared. "May Eiros thrive and be wealthy."

"And may the mighty Lox Empire remain eternally dominant and just," King Malloron

194

returned. He leaned forward. "What is your decision?"

Drocco appreciated his straight-forward approach. "I will take your deal."

Malloron smiled.

"With some amendments," Drocco added.

Malloron's smile faded. "Like what?"

"Firstly, you have been dominating the ports and not allowing traders from the islands fair access. These islands are part of my Empire and their traders have priority. You will pull back."

Malloron nodded. "I wasn't aware of that. Of course."

"With regards to our agreement, I will give you all the knowledge of how I created the Lox in return for your spell, but I will not send you warriors."

Malloron nodded. "Deal."

Drocco eyed him carefully before nodding himself. "Deal."

Malloron stood. "In order to do this now, I'll need to take hold of your portal. Do you permit it?"

Drocco glanced at the group of Talent-crafters behind the portal. They all nodded. "Yes," he replied.

The portal began to glow, and then widen, change color and stretch. After a few moments, it settled back into the shimmer it had been before. "We can now pass items through the portal," Malloron said.

Drocco nodded. He held his hand out to the Talent-crafter who handed him a bundle of parchment. "Give me your spell first," he said to Malloron.

Malloron stood before the portal and lifted a scrap of parchment in his hand. "It's a series of words."

Drocco frowned. He glanced at Torin, who was already discussing it with the crafters. "I do not use the Talent, Malloron," Drocco said. "I cannot cast a spell."

"If you want to be the one to see her history, you have to cast it," Malloron replied. "That is the only way. You don't have to be skilled in order to cast it, you just have to say the words correctly in the Ancient Tongue. The spell is weaved to do the rest of the work."

Out of the corner of his eye, Torin nodded, but Drocco remained silent. He had never thought he would ever use the Talent. Ever. His father had met his end at the hands of a Talent-crafter—in fact, their entire existence when Drocco had been younger had been difficult because of Talent-crafters. He had never once desired being involved with magic in that way.

As he stood considering it, Malloron watched him closely. "I have made it easy for a non-skilled person to cast this, Emperor. It has taken a lot of work on my part. I have hardly slept or ate since we last spoke. If you are concerned, you can have your crafters look at it thoroughly before you give me your part of the bargain." He held out his scrap of parchment, his hand penetrating the portal.

Drocco took the parchment and gave it to Torin, who brought it to the Talent-crafters. As they stared at it, discussing quietly, Malloron stood and waited patiently.

Something about his behavior was disturbing. Drocco watched him closely, but couldn't place the feeling. The parchment came back to him with a nod from his Talent-crafters and Drocco looked over the words.

"How do I cast this?" he asked.

"Make sure you're looking in her eyes," Malloron said. "And say it clear and loud. You will have to memorize it."

Drocco nodded. He pushed his bundle of parchment through the cool silky feel of the portal. "Here is an outline of everything I did to create the Lox. I cannot guarantee it will work for you."

Malloron nodded and took it. "Thank you. I wish you well with your casting, Drocco. I will listen for good news that you have found more Omegas. I'm pleased to consider you an ally."

Drocco nodded. "As am I. Farewell."

Malloron bid him farewell and closed the portal.

Torin approached him as the Talent-crafters left the room again. "That was strange."

"I know," Drocco said, thoughtfully.

"It was too easy—he was too amenable."

Drocco glanced at him. "But the spell is safe?"

Torin nodded. "It seems so. The Talent-crafters say it's a complex spell and it seems safe but they cannot see every thread of it. They wish to examine it further before you use it just in case."

"How long will that take?"

Torin shrugged. "A week, maybe two?"

Drocco thought for a moment. "No. I want to use it immediately."

"Are you sure?"

"Yes. The quicker I know more about her, the quicker I can find the other Omegas. Plus, her Haze is close. Explain this to them and tell them they have three hours to examine it further. Can I cast this even if the charms disabling the Talent are in effect?"

"Since the Talent has been disabled on the floor of your bedroom, the spell may need a charm to protect it from being disabled too. The Talent-crafters have been working on a solution for this since yesterday. They should have something."

When Drocco returned to his bedroom, he was pleased to see the extent of Cailyn's anger. The room was a mess—more so than he had imagined.

He stood by the door scouring the room for her. "Cailyn. Come here."

There was no answer. He peered over to where her nest usually was, but it had been moved about in her frenzy.

"Don't make me come and find you, Cailyn," he warned.

After a long moment, a shuffling came from a corner next to the bed. Cailyn's head appeared as she pulled herself up from a wad of blankets. She looked as though she hadn't slept much either. Her hair was a frazzled mess and the hard look of anger was still on her face. As usual, she looked gorgeous. He stepped through the mess toward her.

"Don't come near me," she snarled.

He kept going until he reached her corner, trying not to smile at how appealing she was when she was angry. He had missed her.

"Don't!" she shouted, as he pulled her out of her nest, like he had done so many times before. "I hate you!" she spat.

He lifted her up into his arms. She tried to resist him but she couldn't make any impact.

"I don't want to smell her on you," she said tightly, fighting him with everything she had.

He shook her a little in annoyance, before holding her tight against him and carrying her across the room, his cock hardening already. "You won't smell anything."

She stilled, her body tense. "You didn't fuck anyone?"

"No."

All of the tension left her body, and she slumped against him allowing him to press her to his chest. "I still hate you."

Drocco chuckled as he cleared a space in the middle of the room. He sat her down on the floor and knelt in front of her. Grabbing her hair, he took her mouth in a hungry kiss, running his hands over her back and up the back of her neck. She kissed him back, but he could sense her resistance. He pulled away to stare into her eyes. "I don't know when you will accept that you are my Omega or that I am your Alpha, but the state of this room confirms it, Cailyn."

She glared at him. "You think that threatening me that you will fuck another will somehow make me agree with you?"

"I had every intention of fucking another," Drocco lied, moving to sit before her. "Something else simply came up."

Her gaze hardened but she didn't say anything.

"I haven't been minding my Empire as I should have been," he added. "I became too busy. It does not invalidate the point that you are angry about the idea of me with another woman. Why is that?"

She remained quiet but her anger was clear, her eyes shiny and hard. In her scent, Drocco could detect again that hint of her Haze. It was approaching. If he was going to apply Malloron's spell, it had to be now.

He settled in front of her. His Talent-crafters had created a charm for him to wear around his neck. It meant that only he could cast within the area that was blocked.

Staring into her eyes, he said, *"Lelah alith sofrey adin-yan mon carrh."*

CHAPTER TWELVE

CAILYN

Cailyn glared at Drocco. She had spent the last day in utter turmoil thinking about him in the throes of ecstasy with another woman, and he had returned so nonchalantly saying he happened to not have time. What a fucking bastard. She couldn't deny she felt some ownership of him, especially his cock, but she had soon come to realize that was the result of the conditioning. The constant fucking and knotting and petting—the scent and sound of him— the way he fed and bathed and groomed her and stayed skin-to-skin with her almost all the time; he had conditioned her to feel better in his presence, and that was why she was having these crazy emotions. He had made her this way.

In the last day since he had been gone, she'd had space to think. Since he had entered the room, after trying to kill her, he hadn't brought any fresh sheets for the bed. No fresh air had entered the room at all. The entire room stank of their sweat, sex, and combined scent—no wonder she had fallen so easily for his conditioning.

She had calmed in the last few hours, managing to get some sleep, but the moment the door opened again, her anger returned full force, even though she knew it was a manipulation. And when he said he hadn't been with another woman, the relief had been almost staggering.

This couldn't continue. She would end up being completely led by her instincts and emotions, which was exactly what he wanted, but what about when he went back to being emperor? He would have made her completely reliant on him and she would end up living the life that she had been trying to avoid— that all of the Omegas had been trying to avoid. And who was to say when he would stop being so amenable? Eventually, he would start questioning her again—no doubt he still wanted to know where the Omegas were, and now it made sense why he had stopped his questioning. He had been manipulating her all along. She fucking hated him.

"Lelah alith sofrey adin-yan mon carrh."

The words shuddered through her, and something changed in the air. For a moment she couldn't place what she was feeling, and then it came to her in a rush.

Magic. Magic had returned.

Drocco looked at her, slight confusion entering his eyes, but she did not wait.

Jumping up, she focused her mind, backing away from him to get some distance so she could focus.

"What is going on?" Drocco muttered, almost to himself.

Focusing, she filtered out as many distractions as she could, and stilled her mind's eye. She called on an enormous amount of magic and gathered it into the space between them, creating a large spear.

As the magic came together, Drocco's eyes widened. He glanced at her and then stood up slowly.

Gritting her teeth and fighting against every instinct that told her it was wrong, Cailyn launched the spear at him at a frightening speed.

He tried to twist out of the way, but couldn't move fast enough, and the spear caught him in the shoulder. It threw him back with incredible force and slammed him back against the wall, pinning him to it. He roared and cursed, his whole body tensing.

A violent tremble rose in Cailyn at the sound of his shock and pain. He was hurt and angry, and needed looking after... She caught herself before her train of thought went too far, and forced herself to turn away from him. She ran to the wardrobe and grabbed a fresh dress, pulling it on as she headed to the window.

"Cailyn!" Drocco thundered. "Where do you think you're going? Stay where you are!"

She faltered in her step, glancing back at him.

He leaned forward into the spear, digging it further into his shoulder, his face contorted.

Cailyn watched for a moment, a worry suddenly gripping her that he would damage himself even further.

"Release me," he ordered her.

Cailyn almost took a step toward him, but quickly stopped. She needed to put her blocks back in place, but couldn't do it now. She stilled her emotions and continued to the window. Casting a spell she used all the time, she unlocked the door leading to the balcony and sucked in a deep breath of fresh air.

"Cailyn!" Drocco's shout shuddered through her, and something about it made her stop.

She turned back to him from the door, taking him in. He had pulled his shoulder along the spear, and away from the wall. Blood soaked his clothing, spreading from the wound. It looked painful, and everything in her wanted to go to him, but she reminded herself that the feelings she was having were not real.

"Do you think I will just allow you to leave?" Drocco bellowed, his eyes wild with anger.

"It will be easier for us both if you just let me disappear," she said, fighting to keep her voice steady.

"Never!" Drocco bellowed. "Wherever you go, I will find you."

"I'll never submit to you the way you want, Drocco."

"Oh, you will," Drocco replied, gritting his teeth as he yanked his shoulder farther down the spear, gouging it deeper as he pushed forward. "After you pay for attacking me, you will do whatever the fuck I want. You think it was bad before? I will destroy you!"

Even as his threat trembled through her, her mind was already clearing now that his scent wasn't in her nose. "No you won't," Cailyn snapped, "because you will never see me again!"

She turned back toward the balcony as the vicious sound of his roar shot through her. Deep in her bones, she knew he was absolutely furious—more than she had ever seen him before. She had to hurry or she would never escape.

Filtering out all noise, she pulled together a thin sheet of magic on the balcony floor. Stepping onto it, she sat down, cross-legged and directed it shakily up into the air. Magic was not supposed to be used to carry weight, but she had no other choice. She wouldn't survive if she went through the palace.

Glancing into the room, she saw Drocco pulling his shoulder free of the spear. She gasped, losing focus, and the magical layer quivered underneath her. Desperate, she calmed her mind and stabilized the magic. Drocco ran toward her and she lifted the layer higher into the air. As Drocco entered the balcony and grabbed for her, she sailed over the railing, just out of his reach. She turned to look at him and they stared at each other as she moved farther away. His eyes burned into her, his face contorted with anger, and his shoulder bloody and ripped. Shame bubbled within her at her actions. She shouldn't have hurt him; it wasn't normal to do that... She blinked and turned away as she sunk into the treetops, cursing her Omega instincts. She had had enough of fighting against them. She maneuvered through the trees and set about installing her blocks back in place, trying to block out the tortured, angry howl tearing through the air from the Alpha she left behind.

The market in the southern part of Ashens city square was busier than she'd ever seen it.

Cailyn navigated straight toward one of the stalls, exhausted from her extensive use of magic and from the physical exertion. She'd had to keep the layer maintained the whole way through the forest—she couldn't afford to leave any clues about where she had gone and the forest floor was too wild for her to step on with her bare feet anyway. After not using the Talent for so long, the considerable use had made her almost incapable of thinking. On top of that, she hadn't actually walked any reasonable distance during the time Drocco had kept her imprisoned; every muscle screamed out for relief.

"Cailyn, what happened?" Dana, an aged market trader came into view, her neat blond hair swept up in a bun.

Cailyn smiled at her, relieved. She stopped, swaying on her feet. "Good to see you again, Dana. It's been a tricky mission."

Dana took her elbow and led her to one of her private booths for clients who wanted to browse goods privately, picking up a pair of sandals and a thick robe on the way.

"I need to speak to the Mothers," Cailyn murmured.

"In time," Dana replied, settling her down onto a thick rug. "You're severely depleted and you smell of..." She hesitated, almost as though she didn't believe what she was about to say.

"I can't wait," Cailyn said. "Please heal me enough to do the spell."

Dana frowned, her wrinkled eyes sweeping over Cailyn. "What the hell happened?"

Cailyn shook her head. "You know I can't tell anyone but the Mothers."

"You reek of Alpha semen," Dana said sharply. "If you have been discovered—"

"I need to speak with the Mothers," Cailyn snapped. "The longer I wait, the worse it will be!"

Dana clamped her mouth shut and moved to stand behind Cailyn, placing her hands on either side of her head.

Cailyn sighed as a cool relief filtered into her brain. As the relief expanded she began to feel stronger, and soon her exhaustion had almost disappeared.

Dana removed her hands. "Do you need help making the portal?"

Cailyn shook her head. "No. I'll be fine, thank you, Dana."

Dana nodded, her blue eyes resting on Cailyn for a long moment before she moved to the mouth of the booth. "Take as long as you need."

Cailyn poured some water from the jug on the table and drank the whole glass before settling back on the rug. She always checked in with the Mothers through a mind portal in Dana's booths when she was in Ashens, but she had no doubt missed a number of check-in times. She didn't know how long it had been—she hadn't even asked Dana—but her break in Ricsford wouldn't have taken so long.

She stilled her body and mind, breathing steadily until her breathing slowed and her heart rate had lowered. Drawing on magic, she created a bubble with a location spell that was aided by the modified magic in the walls of Dana's booth. She directed it into her mind and called out to the Mothers. It took longer than normal for them to respond, which wasn't surprising since they weren't expecting her.

Finally, she felt the pull in her mind and found herself in the familiar briefing room in the Omega Compound. The five white-robed Mothers sat around the curved table, their faces full of varying expressions of concern. She knew they were looking at her mental projection, just as the room was a projection to her, but it felt real in her mind.

"What has happened, Cailyn? Why have you been out of touch for so long?" asked Mother Naysa, the Omega on the far right. "Have you heard the news about an Omega in Lox Palace?"

"Did you manage to see anything while you were there?" Mother Freya asked. "None of our people have been able to confirm if it's true."

Cailyn took a breath, gathering her thoughts for a moment, and then began to tell them what had happened.

The Mothers were much older Omegas, all of whom had been extensively trained as spies and worked for most of their lives protecting Omegas and the Omega Compound. They didn't leave the compound now, but ran it successfully for years. Only one of them, Mother Azia had been there at the start of the growth of the Omega Compound. She had been instrumental in the gathering of Omegas in the Eastern Lands and was at least over one hundred and twenty years old. She sat in the middle of the five and rarely spoke, but was most certainly the wisest and the most ruthless. Either side of her were the two auburn twins, Mothers Freya and Fern, and on either side of them Mothers Naysa and Orlee.

As Cailyn arrived at the point of her captivity, three of the Mothers rose from their chairs, horror on their faces.

"Does he know about us?" Mother Freya asked sharply, interrupting.

"Yes," Cailyn said quietly. "He knows that Omegas have chosen to remove themselves from society because of the brutality of Alphas."

They stared at her, the silence lengthening.

"What else did you say?" Mother Orlee asked.

"That's all he knows," Cailyn insisted. "He doesn't know where you are or anything else about how we navigate the Lands." She continued to explain what had happened and when she finished, the Mothers looked a little calmer and thoughtful. The three that stood, sat back down.

"How did he prevent you from using the Talent?" Mother Naysa asked.

"I don't know," Cailyn admitted. "And I don't know how it came back. He seemed to have spoken a spell that allowed me access again... He didn't seem to know it would do that."

"This is worrying," muttered one of the twins. "If he can stop us using the Talent, it will make things difficult for us."

"We knew he would likely make some discoveries from his acquisition of the palace," Mother Orlee responded. "That's why we sent Cailyn in the first place."

Cailyn kept her eyes on Mother Azia. She had stared down at the table as Cailyn had spoken and hadn't moved. The other Mothers discussed and argued for a few moments about how to deal with Drocco, but Mother Azia seemed to be somewhere else. Cailyn watched Mother Azia closely every time she had any contact with the Mothers, and it was unusual for her to drift away. Finally, Mother Azia moved, and Cailyn was suddenly alert.

Azia rose from her seat, her eyes on Cailyn, and the other Mothers fell silent.

"We will send someone to come and erase your memories of us, Cailyn," Mother Azia said, her raspy voice low. "Go back to your Alpha."

A shot of fear and confusion flooded Cailyn's mind, and the entire projection trembled. "What?"

"He will not let anything happen to you," Mother Azia continued. "If you are the only Omega known publicly, it is better that you are at least an Empress. Of course, if you bear any Omega children, we will take them."

The other Mothers stared at Mother Azia and Cailyn's mouth dropped open, barely believing what she was hearing. "I know I let you down, Mother," Cailyn said, desperately. "I know I let everyone down. But this punishment is extreme."

Mother Azia held her eyes, confusion on her leathery face. "This isn't punishment." She tilted her head. "You have forgotten some of your training, Cailyn. Tell me, do you think your blocks were truly defective against the effects of this Alpha? Even though they worked for everything else?"

Cailyn thought back to her training, desperate to try to please her favorite Mother. As she did so, the faces of the Mothers around the table dropped one by one. The mood shifted to a somber one, Cailyn being the only one to not understand.

"I don't know," she said, finally. "It was something I was going to ask you about."

"You can only be affected by your true mate through the blocks, Cailyn," Mother Naysa said, quietly.

Cailyn stared at her, her face knitting in disbelief. Her true mate? *Drocco* was her true mate? That couldn't be true. "No," she said, in horror. "No, no, no. Absolutely not. You're mistaken, Mother!"

Mother Azia watched her but didn't say anything.

"He didn't…" Cailyn thought back to everything that had happened. "He tortured me. He tried to condition me and use my impulses against me."

Mother Azia turned to leave the room, and Cailyn panicked.

"Mother!" Cailyn called to her, an anger rising. "I will not be cast away. You cannot leave me to suffer at his hand."

Mother Azia froze and turned slowly. The other Mothers were silent, all their eyes downcast.

"Suffer?" Mother Azia said. "Did you mate with him willingly?"

"I didn't want to—"

"Did you kiss him? And encourage him into your body?" Mother snapped.

"I've already explained," Cailyn said. "It was my instincts—"

"It was *you*," Mother Azia said. "Your Omega instincts are you, Cailyn. They are a part of you you rarely experience while you are blocked, but they are still you." She paused, puckering her lips. "I'm sorry that you have not been prepared for this. We devote much of the training to warning Omegas of the threat that Alphas can be that we only briefly touch on the true nature of the Alpha/Omega connection. But you must understand that we are genetically compatible with Alphas. We crave much of their nature. Your reaction to him, to your true mate, is normal."

"No, I was manipulated," Cailyn insisted. "Yes, some of it was my instincts, but much of it was conditioning."

Mother's gray eyes narrowed. "Tell me, did you nest? Did you purr for him? Did you feel ownership of him?"

Cailyn struggled to find a way to answer that didn't seem so incriminating.

"You were comfortable with him, Cailyn." Mother's statement wasn't stated as an accusation, but Cailyn couldn't help but see it as one.

"I nested when he was torturing me," she bit out. "It was the only way to feel safe enough to sleep."

Mother Azia looked at her appraisingly. "The strength of his scent caused you to nest, Cailyn. It caused you to find a way to deal with the pain, and in order to do that you took comfort in his scent."

"No, I didn't," Cailyn said, anger blazing through her. "You were not there, Mother. I did *not* take comfort in his scent. I nested on my own."

"Where did your nest materials come from?"

"His bed." Cailyn suddenly realized the implication and quickly added, "The bed he tortured me on."

Mother nodded. "The bed he soiled with his semen and sweat when he tortured you."

Cailyn opened her mouth to reply but she couldn't. She was stunned and utterly speechless.

All of the Mothers watched her carefully, and suddenly the truth of her situation descended over her. Tears stung her eyes and nose, and she blinked, trying to come to terms with what was happening.

"You are abandoning me," she whispered.

"We have trained you and cared for you and supported you your whole life," Mother Naysa, said gently. "You are one of our best. I don't want to lose you, my daughter, but this cannot be helped. You have to accept change."

"The whole Land has been talking about you—we thought the reports of an Omega in the Palace had been faked to bolster Drocco's support," said Fern quietly. "If it had been any other Alpha, or any other type of connection, we would have had more options before us."

"You have found your true mate, Cailyn," Mother Azia added. "It's something that should be rejoiced. This is no punishment, this is a gift."

"I don't want him."

"You don't get to say that," Mother Azia snapped. "Your life will be filled with pleasures almost no other Omega alive will ever experience. You have already had much that the Omegas in this compound will never have."

"Pleasure isn't everything, Mother," Cailyn said, her voice breaking. They couldn't possibly understand the horror of who he was. "He is cruel, and vicious and is only concerned with conquering every challenge that arises. That's what I am to him. A challenge—something precious only because no one else has it."

"Did you take time to get to know him?" Mother Orlee asked. "To find out why he is the way he is? Did you have any honest and open conversations with him without any hostility, Cailyn? It is easy to judge when you don't understand."

Cailyn stared at her. "Did you hear how he tortured me?"

"Maybe he was as unprepared to deal with your connection as you were," Mother Fern said.

"How can my true mate be someone I despise? Someone I never want to be around? You say you haven't prepared me, but I know enough to know that it isn't normal to hate your true mate."

"Do you hate him?" Mother Fern asked. "Or do you hate his actions? Did you not find anything about him honorable or interesting?"

"It sounds like you don't know him well enough to truly hate him, Cailyn," said Mother Naysa.

Cailyn shook her head in disbelief. How could they be saying this?

"Being true mates doesn't mean you never disagree or fight," Mother Azia said. "It means that you're highly compatible for breeding, it means you're highly attracted to each other and cannot resist each other's nature. It means that you are stronger together, and feel complete with each other.

True mate couples achieve more and live longer. It *is* a gift, Cailyn. Even if you don't think so."

Cailyn lowered her head, tears stinging her eyes. "But he's a monster," she muttered. "How could I be the true mate of someone so..." She couldn't find the word to complete her dejected thought.

"Did he purr for you?"

Cailyn lifted her eyes. Mother Azia had tears in her eyes and Cailyn suspected she too had experienced the purr of an Alpha. "Yes."

"Then you know he isn't a complete monster—he won't be to you. You said he went days without mating you after he attacked you—do you know that goes against his nature? I have known Omegas on their deathbeds still mated and knotted by their Alphas as viciously as if they weren't slipping away from this world. He restrained himself for your comfort and your comfort alone. He waited until you were ready to mate again and then let you lead the way. I would say he was trying to redress his actions, trying to apologize, in that confusing way that Alphas do."

Cailyn was silent for a moment. "He threatened to hurt me when I left," she said, quietly. "He said when he finds me he will do worse than he did before. You're asking me to willingly go back to that."

"He is angry you betrayed him, but he will calm if you return to him," she said. "The longer you are apart, the more vicious he will become. He will not stop until he has you. That's another reason why there is no point in you joining us again—you will put us in danger, especially since he already knows we exist. His memory will have to be modified too, if we can get access to him."

Cailyn took a shaky breath and finally considered the idea. "I don't know if I can really return to him, Mother. I don't know if I can deal with who he is. He wants me to be submissive to him and he is keen to have multiple women for sex… After I left, it seemed like it wasn't really that intense—like it wasn't real."

"I can assure you it was real, Cailyn," Mother said gently. "That kind of bond cannot be faked. It's your blocks making it seem that way. As for who Drocco is… you just need to find a way to tame him for yourself. You have more power than you think. And although he may try, no Alpha will have an interest in any female that isn't his destined Omega once he has met her, and certainly not once he has mated her." Mother Azia smiled as glistening tears dropped onto her cheeks. "Go to your Alpha, my daughter."

Cailyn wandered the market, her mind in turmoil.

Everything the Mothers had said revolved in her mind until one thing became clear; she could not return to the Omega Compound. She would never be able to return. She would never be a spy again, she would never see Victoya or Amara or any of the Mothers. She cried silently as she walked, the market's muddle scents and sounds blurring her senses. Her life had changed so dramatically, and she didn't even know how it happened.

She wandered through the port, along the edge of the sea traders' stalls, wondering how she could possibly return to Drocco. Yes, when it was good, it was fantastic, but it was always a physical thing—their personalities did not match. She was not the submissive he wanted, and he was not the kind of Alpha she would ever have chosen. Still, there was obviously something between them if they were true mates. There had been a spark of potential there when they hadn't spoken for days on end, but was that what being true mates meant? That you didn't speak for fear of upsetting each other? Her mind drifted over what Mother Orlee mentioned—an honest, open conversation. Drocco didn't seem capable of that.

Her tears flowed as she thought back through all her missions, all her training, all of the extensive exercises to skill her Talent—all useless. That life was gone. How could the Mothers discard her so easily? How could they erase all of that knowledge too?

She sighed, turning to head away from the port, when a strong-smelling cloth slammed over her nose and mouth. A number of hands grabbed her and she froze in shock before fighting against their hold. A dizziness swept over her and she lost her balance.

Someone wrapped an arm around her waist, propping her up against their own body.

"Have you got her?" a female voice said to her right.

"Yes, let's go," said the man who held her.

They moved along in silence for a little while and Cailyn could do nothing but allow herself to be half-dragged, half-carried. Her body didn't respond to her instruction and her mind was too blurry to use the Talent, but at least her blocks remained in place. Her mood dropped. Drocco had already found her before she even had the chance to decide.

After a little while, they stopped and the man that held her struck up a conversation with another man, although Cailyn couldn't keep up with what they were saying. Eventually, the man continued to shuffle her forward, passing the man he was just speaking to, and stepping on a bridge that hovered over the distinctive white foamy waves of the White Ocean. Her heart began to pound when she glimpsed the side entrance of an enormous ship at the end of the bridge.

"We leave immediately," said the man they passed.

"Excellent," said the man dragging her toward the ship. "May Eiros thrive and be wealthy."

End of Book One

Turn the page for a sneak preview of the
next book in the series

CRAVE TO CAPTURE

Available now

CHAPTER ONE

DROCCO

"How do you intend to find her now?" Torin asked, as they marched out of the dungeon where the hacked and mutilated bodies of the Lox Talent-crafters lay strewn on the blood-pooled floor. "I know you don't want to have anything to do with the Talent now, Drocco, but they were our best chance of understanding how she could be hiding or traveling."

Drocco gripped the handle of his dripping axe tighter, glaring unseeingly down the corridor and ignoring the pain still aching in his shoulder. It had been the only thing that had stopped him from personally executing the Talent-crafters earlier. His shoulder had needed to be treated, patched up, and given time to heal. Over those days, the Talent-crafters deduced that Malloron's spell destroyed all of the Talent-disabling charms in the palace. But that information did not save them. "They were not our best chance for anything," Drocco said, his voice hard. "They were not as skilled as Malloron, and I have no use for Talent-crafters who are lesser skilled than my enemies."

"You gave them three hours to examine that spell, Drocco," Torin said, evenly. "They asked for at least a week."

"That is of no consequence!" Drocco bellowed, his anger spiking. "They were simply not skilled enough. We need crafters who can protect us from him."

"Agreed," Torin said, his voice low. "But now we have no protection at all."

Drocco halted abruptly and turned to him. "That spell could have killed my Omega, Torin. It could have killed me. It could have done unimaginable things to everyone in this palace. It could have disabled the entire Lox army and left the Empire defenseless."

"Then you should have waited for their assessment," Torin replied, his gray eyes boring into Drocco's. "I know you don't want to hear it, Drocco, but your eagerness for answers is what caused this."

Drocco stepped closer to him, a dangerous glint in his eyes. "The Talent-crafters admitted that they wouldn't have been able to deduce the effects of the spell before it was cast. They couldn't even recreate it in the five days it took to treat my shoulder. No matter when I used it, it would have had the same result, except my Omega may have been pregnant or bonded to me instead, which would have been worse!" The thought drove his anger to a hot peak. "They failed in their duty to the Lox Empire and they suffered the consequences. Do you disagree?"

Torin was quiet. "No."

Drocco turned and continued to march down the corridor, determined to do whatever necessary to find Cailyn.

He knew his fury could be felt across the entire Empire. Households were searched, carriages were stopped, buildings and factories were destroyed, citizens were questioned fiercely and some imprisoned. The Lox descended upon every territory within the Eastern Lands intent on watching everyone and everything, and citizens did not respond well to it, particularly those still loyal to the late King of Ashens. Protests began, and although they were stamped out almost immediately, deaths occurred.

Drocco didn't give a fuck. He wanted Cailyn back. If every single person in the Eastern Lands had to die for that to happen, so be it.

Someone had to have seen Cailyn in Ashens the day she escaped, and he wanted the Empire to feel the pressure until she was found. Of course, no one beyond Torin and his generals knew they were actually searching for his Omega. They only knew that the Lox had an interest in finding a certain female with deep brown eyes and copper-colored hair, who was of great importance to the Empire. Every young woman fitting her description had to be brought in, and Drocco looked upon each one of them himself before allowing any to return to their families. As he sifted through them, Drocco's agitation grew hotter. The longer they took to find her, the farther away she could get, especially now that she could use the Talent again.

❖

Two weeks trickled by and Drocco hardly slept. He spent every waking moment seething that his Omega had dared to attack him, while also battling a desperation to find her that he couldn't control.

She was supposed to be carrying his child and heir by now, not fleeing from him in his own Empire. After she escaped, he sent troops to surround the forest she had disappeared into, but she never appeared. The search of the forest had not resulted in finding her body, which relieved him somewhat, but he couldn't bear the thought that she was roaming the Eastern Lands.

It stung to know that she hadn't softened to him like he'd thought she had. She took the first opportunity to attack and escape. He had allowed himself to believe that their time in his bedroom had been real for her, but instead, he lost himself in her. He said he wouldn't become a fool for Omega pussy, but that was exactly what happened. He had been tricked by how she made him feel and it incensed him that he allowed himself to be deceived by her yet again. If she wasn't going to ever accept him, he should break her like the traitor she was, and keep her imprisoned where she would never see daylight again. And yet the thought caused an uncomfortable twinge in his stomach.

Memories of her tortured him, revolving in his mind constantly; her full lips when she scowled, her expression when she orgasmed, how she bit her lip when she was undecided, and the way she pulled him deeper into her when her legs wrapped around him. He couldn't go back into his bedroom without smelling her fading scent or seeing her nest, where she had purred for him and clung to him like he was the only thing she cared about. How could he turn his back on the possibility of returning to that state with her? And what did that mean for his future? He couldn't see himself settling with an inferior woman to raise his family. He just couldn't.

He and Torin talked over varying theories of why Malloron chose to craft his spell so that it knocked out the defenses Drocco had against the Talent. Drocco, of course, considered it to be intentional, but Torin pointed out that there was no way that Malloron would know that Cailyn was a Talent-crafter. Even the Lox crafters had no idea that she was the one who created the barrier that kept him from her during her Haze. Malloron couldn't have known that she would use the Talent; therefore, there was a possibility that he hadn't intended it or it had done something else that they weren't aware of.

Drocco, however, remained bitter. How could Malloron weave a spell that went so wrong? How could his spell just accidentally leave them vulnerable? He wasn't convinced and Torin had to admit it was suspicious. Either way, they had no way of contacting Malloron now that their Talent-crafters were dead. They arrested and imprisoned all of the Western Land traders that were in the Empire. Most of them worked at the port borders and so their ships were held too. Perhaps once Malloron's precious trading stopped being profitable, he would contact them.

Torin strengthened the security around the palace and increased Drocco's guard, but Drocco didn't care about any of that. With the mood he was in, he would gladly cut down anyone who dared to even look at him too closely.

As three weeks drew to a close, Drocco spent a lot of time at the Records Keep looking through the Omega research on the top floor. The details that the keeper had put together for him was thorough and wide-ranging, from Omega accomplishments across the Lands to typical pregnancy behaviors. It was fascinating and he found himself reading more deeply.

At the start of the fifth week, Torin arrived at the keep unannounced.

"I'm sorry to disturb you, Drocco," he said, eyeing the many files and parchment sheets laying around the table, chairs, and floor. "But I have some witnesses for you that cannot wait."

Drocco rose from his chair. "Bring them in."

Torin nodded at the door, and three men of different ages stumbled into the room, their ankles restricted by shackles and their wrists bound together. They wore simple, faded clothes and their skins looked weathered. An odd smell wafted from them and they trembled as they saw Drocco.

"You are sea traders?" Drocco guessed.

They nodded, their eyes wide.

"Tell him what you told me," Torin ordered.

The youngest of the three swallowed and took a breath. "We work on the sea border, your Imperial Majesty, and there's always... people bein' traded on them big ships that go to the Western Lands."

Drocco's eyes narrowed. "Yes, and?"

"I'm sure I saw…" He glanced at the other men, who nodded at him. "We saw a woman of the description you're looking for being carried onto one of them ships."

A fierceness gripped Drocco. "How long ago?"

"Going on five weeks, now," said another, older man with a chunky square beard. "She was wearing the exact dress your Lox warriors have been askin' about—black with the red collar, and red stitching on the sleeves. Her hair was wild an' curly too."

"The only reason why we noticed her," added the third and graying man, "was because she seemed unconscious. Since you came into power, your Imperial Majesty, they stopped druggin' people. Most of the slaves are chained and led onto them ships, but she was being carried. We noticed it and commented that maybe things were goin' back to how they used to be, and then continued on with our work."

Drocco exhaled a breath, a raw anger clawing through his mind, through his every muscle. If she had to be drugged and carried onto the ship, she had not gone willingly. "What ship was it?"

"We think it was one of the big slaver ships from Eiros," chunky beard replied. "It was blue—" He turned to the other men who nodded in confirmation. "—and the big blue ships are usually from there."

Torin began speaking and the shackles clanged, but Drocco couldn't pay attention to what was going on, only one thought dominated his mind; Malloron had taken Cailyn. He had dared to use the Talent to steal Drocco's Omega. Maybe he did know she used the Talent—maybe he didn't. Either way, if he could organize her capture so quickly after her escape, he had planned it. It explained everything; why he had been so amenable, why he had taken the deal, why he hadn't yet contacted them about his traders being imprisoned. He had an Omega... Drocco's Omega. That bastard thought he could challenge Drocco in this way and nothing would come of it? Drocco had no idea the man could be so fucking stupid.

"Do you want to kill all of his people that we hold?" Torin asked, quietly.

Drocco blinked, reemerging from his dark thoughts. "No," he said. Turning on his heels, he left the Records Keep and headed back to the palace.

"Lox!" Drocco's address boomed out across the Great Hall. His army of Alpha quietened and looked up at him expectantly. After spending so long searching for this particular female, they were clearly eager to know what was going on. "Our enemy across the White Ocean, King Malloron, has done the unthinkable," Drocco spat, his anger bubbling in him. "He has dared to use the Talent to steal my Omega, your future Empress."

A vicious blast of exclamations burst into the hall.

"She presented herself to me, in her Haze, in front of Lox warriors and rulers of territories in the Empire—she is obviously mine," Drocco bellowed over the din. "She is our best method of finding the rest of the Omegas, but she is also the mother of future heirs to the Empire you secured. And

Malloron had her drugged and forced onto a ship heading for Eiros."

The warriors before him snarled and bellowed and gnashed in disbelief, becoming louder as their anger built, shifting on their feet with outrage. The discord made the entire hall buzz with a harshness that matched Drocco's mood.

"I do not know what King Malloron seeks to do with her," he shouted, a dark tone in his voice, "but I am declaring war on Eiros."

The hall erupted. Roars and yells came at Drocco from all angles. He held his palm up until the noise quietened somewhat.

"Obviously the Empire is still under reconstruction, and it would be unwise for it to be left unattended, so some of you will be remaining here to guard what I leave behind." He lowered his voice. "And I expect my Empire to still stand when I return."

The noise rose again, chuckles among the calls requesting to go with him.

"We crushed many kings on our way to our victory, and now we will crush another," Drocco shouted, clenching a fist and rising it into the air. "We are Lox! And we will remain eternally dominant and just."

His warriors' roars blasted at him with the same ferocity of raw anger that burned within him. Drocco snarled back at them, a dark anticipation settling within him. He was going to enjoy destroying that bastard Malloron and he was going to enjoy teaching his Omega the consequence of running from him, as soon as she was back in his bed, where she belonged.

~

Author Note

This story was a bit of a tidal wave for me. I'm a planner—I like to organize and forward-think, and do all that stuff most people think is boring, but this came upon me in a rush, with the sparking of an idea and the suggestion to tackle my own version of an Omegaverse. Once that spark took hold, I couldn't stop world-building and plotting and figuring out who these characters were, and pretty soon I was compelled to write it. I had no idea I was going to be writing this even a month before I started and I've never had that happen to me before! But I loved, loved, loved the process.

This book won't be for everyone. There are contrasting elements that don't always sit together; M/F Omegaverse (with knotting beings), a dark romance (with a couple who cannot understand each other), in an epic fantasy world (with magic)… the only thing missing is dragons! But it is exactly the story I wanted to tell.

Even though this is an Omegaverse, my number one inspiration for this work was The Golden Dynasty by Kirsten Ashley. I absolutely love that book—I think it's probably my favorite romance book of all time—and it helped me to see that romance can be the feature of a story in an Epic Fantasy setting, and it can be complex, and steamy, and raw, and brutal. The Omegaverse element is what brought the final details of this story together, for me. The power struggle and conflict typical to Omegaverse stories suited my initial dark romance idea so much that it kinda slotted into place almost fully formed. I wasn't able to make sense of the story without that defining element, and being a PNR fan, the animistic nature of the dynamics felt natural. Plus, I do love a 'true mates' story :) I hope to continue to create more stories that fall within my own brand of Dark Epic Fantasy Romance.

If you enjoyed this book, I'm so glad to have found you! If you know anyone else who would enjoy it, please recommend it to them. If you didn't enjoy it, I'm sure you'll find something to love in your next read. Either way, thank you for giving it a chance, and please consider leaving a review wherever you bought the book so other readers know what they're getting into if they decide to try it.

P.S. If you did love the story, come over to my reader's group, Dark Halos, where I can keep you updated and feed you loads of dark, erotic treats :D

Acknowledgments

Randie; thank you for coming with me on this much darker ride! Ha! I'm so glad all my warnings didn't put you off, I love working with you. Once again, your great editing skills have improved my words and I can't thank you enough for your constant support and enthusiasm for my work. Thank you, thank you, thank you!

L; you deserve a stiff drink for dealing with all my moaning and whining! Thank you for slapping me out of my self-doubt, helping me with my obsession over names and content concerns, and banning me from reading when 'comparison-itis' almost made me scrap this—I know it was all for your own benefit so you could get your grabby little hands on Drocco, but I'm thankful anyway LOL! I hope this book is everything you imagined. Of course, Drocco is all yours… except when he's mine ;)

Nora; this is all your fault! Ha ha ha! Thank you for your encouragement to tackle omegaverse, I never would have considered it otherwise. You're such a great inspiration and I appreciate all your kind words and encouragement. :D Thanks so much for your support.

To the readers who decided to take a chance on this book, thank you so much. I loved building this world and hope you enjoyed spending time in it. There's more to come! Drocco and Cailyn aren't done yet :)

Lastly, a massive thanks to all of my friends and family, who consistently encourage me on this journey. I love you guys.

~ Zoey Ellis ~